HALIFAX HAUNTS

*Exploring the City's
Spookiest Spaces*

HALIFAX HAUNTS

Exploring the City's
Spookiest Spaces

STEVE VERNON

NIMBUS
PUBLISHING

Nimbus Publishing Limited
PO Box 9166 Halifax, NS B3K 5M8
WWW.NIMBUS.CA
(902) 455-4286

Printed and bound in Canada
Nimbus Publishing is committed to protecting our natural environment. As part
of our efforts, this book is printed on 100% recycled content stock.

Design: John van der Woude
Front cover design: Heather Bryan
Author photo: Belinda Ferguson
Photography: Steve Vernon

Library and Archives Canada Cataloguing in Publication Data

Vernon, Steve
Halifax haunts : exploring the city's spookiest spaces / Steve Vernon.
ISBN 978-1-55109-707-7

1. Ghosts—Nova Scotia—Halifax. 2. Haunted places—Nova Scotia—Halifax.
3. Ghost stories, Canadian (English). 4. Halifax (N.S.)—History. I. Title.
BF1472.C3V46 2008   133.109716'22   C2008-907382-7

We acknowledge the financial support of the Government of Canada through
the Book Publishing Industry Development Program (BPIDP) and the Canada
Council, and of the Province of Nova Scotia through the Department of
Tourism, Culture and Heritage for our publishing activities.

Home

will always haunt you

no matter where you hang your hat

Halifax Harbour

ANGUS L. MACDONALD BRIDGE

8

4

7

5

6 3

2

UPPER WATER STREET

LOWER WATER STREET

HOLLIS STREET

NORTH STREET

BARRINGTON STREET

9

BRUNSWICK STREET

DUKE STREET

13

16

17

14

15

10

BARRINGTON STREET

11

12

18

20

CITADEL HILL

SACKVILLE STREET

19

21

SPRING GARDEN ROAD

MORRIS STREET

22

ROBIE STREET

27

28

23

SOUTH PARK STREET

QUINPOOL ROAD

JUBILEE ROAD

COBURG ROAD

UNIVERSITY AVENUE

SOUTH STREET

OXFORD STREET

26

25

Northwest Arm

29

GEORGES
ISLAND
1

Roach
Cove

WINDMILL ROAD

33

A MURRAY MACKAY BRIDGE

The Narrows

Bedford Basin

BEDFORD HIGHWAY

32

Birch
Cove

31

WINDSOR STREET

JOSEPH HOWE DRIVE

BAYERS ROAD

DUNBRACK STREET

BICENTENNIAL ROAD

30

POINT PLEASANT PARK

24

1	George's Island
2	The Brewery Market
3	Maritime Museum of the Atlantic
4	Sea Serpent Sighting at Halifax Harbour
5	Halifax Ferry Terminal
6	Lower Water Street
7	Historic Properties
8	The Angus L. Macdonald Bridge
9	Little Dutch Church
10	Halifax Alehouse
11	Halifax Citadel
12	Citadel Hill Tunnels
13	Halifax City Hall
14	The Five Fishermen
15	St. Paul's Church
16	The Halifax Club
17	Neptune Theatre
18	Spring Garden Road Memorial Public Library
19	The Old Courthouse
20	St. Paul's Cemetery
21	Waverley Inn
22	Holy Cross Cemetery
23	Victoria General Hospital
24	Point Pleasant Park
25	Shirreff Hall
26	University of King's College
27	Robie Street Witch's House
28	The Cathedral Church of All Saints
29	Deadman's Island
30	Ashburn Golf Club (Old Course)
31	Fairview Lawn Cemetery
32	Prince's Lodge
33	Navy Island

Contents

Preface

———————————

Back in 2004 when I put together my first ghost story collection, *Haunted Harbours: Ghost Stories from Old Nova Scotia*, I was astounded at just how many ghost stories there were in this province. I had to leave an awful lot out. I put together a second collection, *Wicked Woods: Ghost Stories from Old New Brunswick*, and I had just as much trouble choosing from the many wonderful New Brunswick tales out there.

So when the folks at Nimbus asked me what I had lined up next, I decided that I'd make things easier by restricting myself to the stories of the city I live in—Halifax. I figured this would be simple: I thought the research would involve very little shoe leather and that I would have no problem picking and choosing. After all, how many Halifax stories could there be?

Shows you what I know. I've collected nearly three-dozen stories in this collection and I still had to leave some out. Putting this collection together took a lot more work than either of my first two collections because I decided to write the book as a do-it-yourself ghost tour.

Why?

Maybe my eyes just naturally tear up and blur painfully at the sight of hairy-legged men in kilts. Mind you, I have worn a kilt, and I have given (and attended) a few ghost walks in my time. As a collector of ghost stories, I find such opportunities offer tailor-made market research.

I still remember the first time I heard a local ghost walk guide retelling my version of "The Piecemeal Ghost of Black Rock Beach."

"Where did you hear that story?" I asked the guide.

"I read it in the newspaper just a few years ago," he told me.

The two of us had a good laugh when I revealed that I had supplied a version of the story to that particular newspaper reporter. Now, I wasn't bothered by the idea of another storyteller telling my story. I had heard it from someone else myself.

That's how it happens. You catch a story the same way you catch a cold—generally, from somebody else. It is the nature of storytelling that your work will be echoed by other folks working in the field. Still, I thought to myself then that I might want to conduct my own ghost walk someday. I made plans to start one in the summer of 2007, but fate intervened. I broke my leg. How did I break it, you ask? Well let's just say that I discovered gravity in an awfully sudden fashion.

So over the spring of 2007, as I lay there contemplating a leg cast that was a fair bit uglier than any hairy, kilted leg imaginable, I got to thinking about this book.

So What is this Book All About?

Good cooks will empty the fridge any chance they get. Onions, sausage, greens, and beans—into the soup pot they will go. I have done the same with this collection by weaving history, folklore, and plain-old storytelling into a kaleidoscopic mixture of ghosts, legends, and dark Halifax history.

I have selected some of the darkest locations I could find in Halifax and have done my level best to unearth every shadowy secret and tale. Believe me, there were a lot of them to choose from. I will warn you that unlike my first two collections, there's a lot more history and fact than campfire smoke in this collection. Not all of these stories are specifically ghost stories, but I guarantee there's enough gore, gossip, and gunpowder in these pages to satisfy a reader's every need.

I've included a map in this book with the story-sites clearly marked, and the order that the story-sites appear in the book should make them easy to follow on foot. The entire route is far longer than anyone could walk, though, even if he or she possessed ten-league boots. So I recommend breaking the sites down into bite-sized chunks. You don't have to try and hit every story-site in this book at a single go.

I begin each section with a short, bare-bones recounting of the story so that you can use the book as a guide rather than having to pause at each site to read through several pages of storytelling. There's nothing wrong with storytelling; however, if you're on a time limit, I've given you a shortcut.

I'd like to thank Patrick Murphy, Dan Soucoup, Caitlin Drake, Terrilee Bulger, Diane Faulkner, Penelope Jackson, and all of the other wonderful folks at Nimbus who have once again shown their faith in me. I'd like to apologize for forgetting your names and faces at every literary function and coffee shop that we meet in.

Thanks to the good folks at the Writers' Federation and at the schools who allow me to entertain and educate students through the Writers in the Schools program.

I'd like to thank all of those great booksellers out there who allow me to sign and peddle my books at their stores. If you folks weren't out there, where would my words wind up?

Thanks are also due to the folks at the Atlantic Canadian Geocaching Association for all their help rounding up the GPS coordinates. Thanks to Brian Shaw, 3 Geeks Outdoor store, Darren "Durango" McKay, Pete "Petemoss" Shacklock, Chris "fishing fanatic" Bowyer, Matthew "Publishing Tin" Bradbury, and Scott Melvin.

And lastly, as always, I'd like to dedicate this novel to my wife, Belinda. She keeps the lantern burning bright and a candle in the window no matter how dark the shadow that I prowl.

George's Island

HALIFAX HARBOUR (ACROSS FROM PIER 21)

N 44°38.45' W 63°33.58'

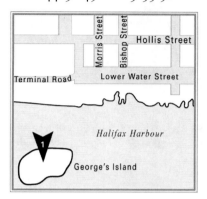

Duc d'Anville's Missing Heart

FOR THE LAST 150 YEARS, A GHOST DRESSED IN THE UNIFORM OF AN eighteenth-century French admiral has been seen walking across the harbour from George's Island and down the streets of Halifax. Some say this spectral sailor is the ghost of Duc d'Anville, a French officer who led an invasion fleet to George's Island only to meet his final fate there.

The Island Itself

As you leave Pier 21, hang a hard-right turn, walk past the Nova Scotia College of Art and Design Port Campus, and aim yourself towards the statue of Sir Samuel Cunard. Just before you reach the Harbourwalk gate, turn right again at the end of the buildings. There's an iron-barred fence separating the land from the sea, and if you look through those bars you'll catch a look at George's Island, a little pimple of dirt and rock about the length of a good-sized cruise ship.

As far as I'm concerned, staring through iron bars is really the only proper way to look at George's Island.

Why? Let me tell you.

In the nine years between 1755 and 1764, nearly ten thousand uprooted Acadians were imprisoned upon this tiny chunk of real estate. Their belongings were taken from them and many were forced to live like animals on the open beaches where they awaited deportation for weeks at a time.

Over the years, George's Island has also served as a quarantine station, a military base, and a graveyard. Back in the seventeenth century, they called the island *Île Raquette*, or "Snowshoe Island."

Relatively small, compared to this cruise ship,
George's Island has played a large role in Nova Scotian history.

Take a look at George's Island from the air and you'll see what I mean. It looks a little like the Native spirit-trickster Glooscap might have dropped an old-fashioned bear paw snowshoe smack-dab in the middle of the harbour.

An Invasion Plan

Let's turn back to the early eighteenth century.

After losing the fortress of Louisbourg to a besieging army of British volunteers and amateur soldiers back in 1745, the French decided to counterattack by sending a fleet to retake the fortress. On the sleepy Sunday morning of June 22, 1746, a French armada of sixty-five ships was dispatched from Rochelle under the command of Admiral Jean-Batiste, de Roye de La Rochefoucauld, otherwise known as Duc d'Anville.

The armada was to sail the Atlantic and land in Halifax Harbour where they were to meet up and reinforce the Mi'kmaq and French forces that were waiting there for them. From there, the armada would organize an invasion of Louisbourg, sack Annapolis Royal, and while they were at it, swing down to burn Boston to the ground.

At least that was the plan.

However, two major storms delayed the fleet for over three months. Bad water and spoiled food didn't help matters much. An outbreak of typhus and the loss of several ships around Sable Island sealed the expedition's fate. By the time they hit Halifax, the Mi'kmaq and French forces that had been waiting for them had given up and gone hunting.

Duc d'Anville's men were ready to give up too. They landed on George's Island and built a hospital out of broken masts and tattered sails. One of the first patients was Duc d'Anville himself. He keeled over during the morning inspection. Some thought he had been poisoned by a disgruntled crew member, but after an autopsy the ship's surgeon declared his death to be apoplexy, which back then was just a fancy way of saying, "Beats me what happened. The guy just dropped down dead."

After some dispute, the ship's doctor decided to perform one of the world's first heart transplants—cutting Duc d'Anville's heart out and sealing it in wax in a small biscuit tin. The wax-covered heart was eventually transported back to France where it was handed over with some ceremony to Duc d'Anville's wife and three children. How'd you have liked to have been the one to unwrap that little souvenir from the colonies, eh?

The Aftermath

On the Wednesday morning of September 17, 1746, a priest and a few officers, and a hastily conscripted burial party carried Duc d'Anville's coffin through the rocky trail to a lonely little spot shaded by a couple of hardy birch trees, where they quickly buried him. The mood of the crew was unpredictable. There was no time to waste on ceremony.

Duc d'Anville's authority as admiral of the invasion fleet was promptly handed over to his second-in-command, Vice Admiral d'Estournelle, who arrived with four more ships of the line on the same day Duc d'Anville died. This fellow took one look about him and decided that the situation was hopeless.

"We must retreat back to France," d'Estournelle declared. "We cannot stay."

"Retreat is not an option," the officers of his staff replied.

A few days later, d'Estournelle, frustrated by the poor morale of his crew and the logistical difficulties of getting supplies shipped to them, dramatically stood up in the middle of an official meeting.

"All is lost," he said. "It is impossible."

He went to his cabin and locked the door. No one dared disturb him. He was still the admiral, after all. Later that evening, moans were heard coming from d'Estournelle's cabin. Members of the ship's crew broke down d'Estournelle's door only to find him lying stretched on the floor in a sea of his own blood. He had thrown himself upon his sword attempting unsuccessfully to take his own life.

Shortly afterward, several of the armada's ships were lost to a storm in the harbour, and fever continued to take its toll. The remainder of the armada sailed back to France in late October. Over 1,800 French sailors and soldiers died in that ill-fated expedition. Three years later, when Cornwallis and his settlers sailed into the harbour in 1749, they too took shelter on Île Raquette and promptly renamed it George's Island, after King George II. The British settlers were terrified by their early discovery of several skeletons still dressed in the tattered rags of the French army.

Later that summer, a French warship, *Le Grande Saint Esprit* sailed into Halifax Harbour and dug up the remains of Duc d'Anville. The location of the grave was a little uncertain; however, the identity of the corpse they dug up was confirmed by the presence of a pig's tooth. It seems Duc d'Anville had a rotten tooth that a crafty French dentist had yanked and replaced with a small pig's tooth.

The *Le Grande Saint Esprit* transported Duc d'Anville's coffin up to Louisbourg, the fortress he had come so far to conquer, which had been ceded back to the French thanks to a 1748 treaty. Duc d'Anville was finally reburied with full military honours at the foot of the high altar in the Louisbourg chapel.

However, the story doesn't end there.

The Ghost of Duc d'Anville

Since his death, there have been dozens of sightings of a mysterious figure in Napoleonic naval dress that walks from George's Island and heads towards town. It has long been believed that this ghost is the ghost of Duc d'Anville.

Folks claim that the spectre is nearly ten feet tall. The spectral figure walks the shoreline to Centennial Park, just beyond Mount Saint Vincent University, to linger close to the Duc d'Anville Monument, which was raised there to commemorate the site where Duc d'Anville's men made camp shortly after his death.

There have been so many sightings of Duc d'Anville over the years that in the late nineteenth century, the Nova Scotia government commissioned an actual scientific study into the veracity of such claims. The study proved inconclusive, however, and the mystery of the Duc d'Anville's wandering ghost lives on in Halifax to this day.

There has been at least one other report of someone claiming to have seen the burial party of the Duc d'Anville rowing up to George's Island and carrying a casket into the shadows. As well, folks who live close to the Bedford Basin claim that on nights when the spirit of Duc d'Anville walks the harbour, you can hear the creaking of tall masts and ropes and sails flapping idly in the Atlantic breeze.

Others claim to have heard the ghost's footsteps echoing through the streets on foggy Halifax evenings, and it's also said that if you get close enough and listen, you can hear the wind whistling through the open wound where the drum of Duc d'Anville's heart once beat.

The Brewery Market

1496 LOWER WATER STREET

N 44°38.650' W 63°34.195'

The Ghost of Alexander Keith

B REWERY EMPLOYEES HAVE SEEN THE GHOST OF ALEXANDER KEITH prowling the tunnels and hallways of his old estate on Lower Water Street. In addition, there have been reports of a screaming man, his face all covered in blood, whose visage has been seen staring out of a men's room mirror.

The building has undergone substantial renovation, and the exact location of that particular men's room has been lost to memory, so all of you weak-bladdered gentlemen might just want to cross your legs and think dry-type thoughts until you move on to a location with a less-haunted men's room.

Where Halifax Began

Once upon a not-so-long time ago, Lower Water Street was exactly where Halifax began and the ocean ended.

How is that you ask?

The fact is, if you are standing on Lower Water Street, then you are standing on what used to be the very edge of Halifax.

Back in 1749, when Lieutenant Colonel Edward Cornwallis and that rowdy band of 2,600 settlers first clambered ashore from the HMS *Sphinx* onto Halifax's coast, this was where the beach began. There was nothing much out here back then but dense, mosquito-ridden woods and a long, steep climb up towards what would eventually become known as Citadel Hill.

Back then they called this harbour *Chebucto*—a mispronounced Mi'kmaq term that roughly translated as "the biggest harbour." And that's just what Halifax Harbour was back then. It was the biggest harbour in the area and perhaps even in the entire continent. The French and the English had previously ignored the harbour simply because it was too big to be practical.

You see, back in those days, the smaller harbours, no bigger than knotholes, were preferred. If you were a sailor or a sea pilot, you would have wanted to find yourself just enough harbour room to dart into if you were being pursued by privateers or poor weather. However, when Cornwallis landed here in 1749, all of that changed.

Many of the settlers were the dregs of the London slums. They were folks who had heard about the promise of free land and a free trip to a brand-new country and thus accompanied Cornwallis to this new country hoping to start a brand-new life. Not everyone planned to stay here. Many used the free transportation Cornwallis's fleet provided to slip away to New England and the promise of America. Others took advantage of the promise of free provisions. Hey, who among you couldn't go for free groceries for a year?

They landed on the edge of Lower Water Street where the shore began.

The shore didn't last, though.

From the turn of the nineteenth century onwards, the piers gradually extended out and the spaces between the piers were filled in with concrete and gravel. The streets ranging from Lower Water Street to the Halifax waterfront are all built upon the ocean. You bear that in mind the next time you walk down to the ferry terminal for a breath of fresh air—you are walking where lobsters used to crawl.

Once these settlers reached the shore, they weren't all that interested in clearing the land about the harbour. The trees that clumped about the coast were too darned hard to cut down and the mosquitoes and blackflies were too carnivorous. No sir, the bulk of these new settlers were more interested in sitting in the shade and sipping on a cold mug of ale and chewing on free groceries. It's no wonder some of the first buildings built as Halifax was slowly and carefully hacked out of the Chebucto woods were taverns.

And this brings us to Alexander Keith.

The Pride of Nova Scotia

Born in Scotland on October 5, 1795, Alexander Keith immigrated to Canada in 1817. Three years later he founded the Alexander Keith's brewing company and developed his signature India Pale Ale, and in 1837 he built the facilities that we can see today here at 1496 Lower Water Street. The building is constructed out of Nova Scotia ironstone. A tunnel connected the brewery to Keith Hall so that the good Mr. Keith could slip down to the brewery any chance he got. Keith was a careful, watchful man; he was a bit of a control freak and was truly obsessed with brewing good beer.

Legend has it that the ghost of Alexander Keith still haunts the building, perhaps making certain that everything is running smoothly in his brewery. Night watchmen hear the sounds of disembodied running footsteps scampering through the hallways at night.

A janitor swears to have seen the visage of a screaming man, covered in blood, in one particular men's room mirror. This claim has been verified by several other Keith's employees over the years since the first mirror sighting.

As far as I know, none of these employees were under the influence of Nova Scotia's finest ale at the time.

The storefront to the Alexander Keith's brewery

Another Ceremony

Alexander Keith is remembered in another fashion as well.

Grateful students regularly pay homage to Alexander Keith at his final resting place in the Camp Hill Cemetery, between Robie Street and Summer Street, on the west side of the Public Gardens.

The GPS coordinates for the gravestone are N 44 38.560 W 63 35.147. I recommend entering the graveyard at the entrance close to the intersection of Sackville Street and Summer Street. If you follow the markers that point toward Joseph Howe's burial site, you will pass directly beside Alexander Keith's final resting place. It is a tall, red marble obelisk, close to the center of the graveyard, and one of the tallest monuments in the whole cemetery. Furthermore, there's almost always an empty bottle of Keith's ale resting beside the stone where some university student or thirsty pilgrim has left it standing upon the gravesite as a small thank you to the man who made Nova Scotia the home of fine ale.

Maritime Museum of the Atlantic
1675 LOWER WATER STREET

N 44°38.86′ W 63°34.26′

Double Alex, Come Again?

M USEUM STAFF MEMBERS HAVE REPORTED LIGHTS SWITCHING on and off, unexplained creaks and groans, and the sound of footsteps echoing through the halls. Objects have been seen moving by themselves, and the shape of a man has been spotted walking through the shadowed hallways. The staff members blame these occurrences on the ghost of Double Alex and a haunted lighthouse lantern. You will find the lantern located just beyond the information desk, directly in front of the parrot cage. Say hello to Merlin the parrot, if he's in a talkative mood.

A Drinking Problem

The Maritime Museum of the Atlantic was founded in 1948. After several relocations, they made a permanent home here on Lower Water Street on the site of the historic William Robertson and Son Ship Chandlery in 1982. However, this story actually began back in the year 1758 when a lighthouse was commissioned to be built upon Sambro Island at the mouth of Halifax Harbour. The light was fuelled by whale oil and eventually kerosene.

The Maritime Museum on Lower Water Street is home to a rather spooky lighthouse lantern.

In 1833, a unit of light artillerymen was stationed on the island to help man the light and operate the signal bells and cannons that were necessary to help ships navigate through the foggy Atlantic water. One day the commander of the unit sent his quartermaster sergeant into Halifax to pick up the unit's payroll.

And that's when the trouble began.

The quartermaster sergeant was named Alex Alexander, or as his fellow soldiers called him—Double Alex. I figure either Alex's parents had one wicked sense of humour or else they stuttered. Whatever the reason, one wonders if his double-barrelled echo of a name was the true reason why Double Alex drank so heavily, or perhaps he just had a taste for Nova Scotia's finest ale.

The drinking came to a head when Double Alex spent the unit's payroll in a Halifax tavern. He woke up under arrest and absolutely penniless. The captain of the unit locked him in the lighthouse for the night. In a fit of shame and depression, Double Alex hanged himself from the large iron cradle that held the lighthouse light.

For years after, Double Alex's ghost was seen around the lighthouse. Kegs were overturned and doors slammed unexpectedly. Even up until the mid-1960s the lighthouse keeper reported hearing footsteps behind him in the fog. The keeper swore that the footsteps belonged to no one other than Quartermaster Sergeant Alex Alexander.

"Who else but a ghost would want to stay in a lighthouse?" the keeper asked.

In 1968, the Sambro Light was completely modernized and a powerful, new electric-powered light replaced the old oil-lit lamp. The old Sambro lighthouse lens was given over to the keeping of the Maritime Museum of the Atlantic. In 1982, when the museum opened the doors to its brand-new Lower Water Street digs, the Sambro Light welcomed visitors into the museum. Following the opening, museum employees reported hearing strange noises and some claimed they had seen the spirit of a man dressed in nineteenth-century military garb.

The museum blames the creaking and stirring noises on the sounds of an old building settling. Still, museum employees don't like to work all that late for fear of encountering the ghost of Double Alex.

When I told my wife, Belinda, that I was adding this story to my collection, she surprised me by admitting that she'd never heard the tale of Double Alex before.

"So that big, old lighthouse light in the museum lobby is supposed to be haunted?" she asked.

I assured her that it was indeed supposed to be.

"You know," she said. "I have seen that light several times on my visits to the museum and it has always given me the creeps. I can't bring myself to even stand too close to it without shivering."

Halifax Harbour

N 44°38.87' W 63°34.04'

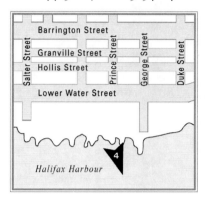

Sea Serpent Sightings

I N 1752, A HALIFAX FISHERMAN CAUGHT A GIANT SEA TURTLE-LIKE creature just outside of the harbour, near the spot where the Sambro Lighthouse now stands—the very same lighthouse where poor Double Alex hung himself. The story was documented in the *London Magazine* and similar sightings have resurfaced over the years.

A Fish Story

The "Monthly Chronicle" column of the August 1752 issue of *London Magazine* tells of a fisherman's unlikely catch that was displayed to the public for a time in Halifax Harbour.

"We caught it just outside the harbour," a fisherman said.

The beast was described as a giant sea turtle, a female of the kind, whose body was about the size of a large ox. I'm not certain how they decided it was female. Perhaps they just peeked between the fins.

The beast was covered with short brownish hair, the consistency of hog's bristle. The skin, very loose and rough, was nearly an inch and a half in thickness. Its neck was short and thick like that of a bull, and the head of the beast was small in proportion and looked very much like that of an alligator.

In the sea beast's upper jaws were two teeth of about nine or ten inches long. The teeth crooked downwards like the tusks of a sabre-toothed tiger. The legs of the sea beast were short and thick and ended with fins and claws like those of a sea turtle. The stomach of the sea beast was exposed as if it had been bitten open. The guts of the thing were said to resemble that of a horse or an ox.

The fisherman displayed the creature for a small fee until the reek of the thing forced him to return it to the depths from which he had hauled it. I guess you might say that the turtle had a smell as well as an outer shell.

I sometimes wonder about what it must have been like to reel in a catch like that. When I see those old men and young boys fishing for mackerel down by the waterfront and not really caring if they catch anything stronger than a mild cold, I sometimes wonder just what they'd think of a catch like this one?

A Second Serpent Sighting

"There's something out there," a boy called out.

It was a sunny Friday on July 15, 1825, when something resembling a sea serpent was spotted in the waters of Halifax Harbour by three separate and independent witnesses. The witnesses were a young man and several young ladies in a carriage on George Street, a farmer named Goreham as well as his family and servants, and a fisherman called William Barry and several of his fishing buddies.

All three of these parties spotted a strange serpentine beast twisting in the waves just beyond the pier directly behind the current location of the Maritime Museum. The beast held its head nearly three feet out of the water. Its body was described as being as big as a large tree trunk, and most of the onlookers agreed that it stretched a good sixty feet in length.

William Barry, the fisherman, swore he counted eight individual humps or coils protruding from out of the water.

"It moved in a sort of writhing motion," he swore. "In and out over the waves."

And then it was gone.

Halifax Harbour is home to many sea serpent sightings.

A Modern-Day Sighting

In the early summer of 2003, Wallace Cartwright headed to sea to check the condition of his lobster traps. The native of Alder Point, Cape Breton County, saw what he thought was a big log in the water. The "log" had a head similar to a sea turtle with a brown, snake-like body. It was approximately twenty-six feet long and had smooth skin.

"I was kind of leery of approaching it," he told CBC Radio. "God knows, the thing might have been able to jump out of the water, you know?"

Cartwright and his assistant watched the creature submerging and surfacing for about forty-five minutes or so. Cartwright, a fisherman for thirty years, stated that what he had seen was unlike anything he had ever encountered before.

"It had a head on it like a sea turtle and it had a body like a snake... about as big around as a five-gallon bucket."

Andrew Hebda, curator of zoology at Halifax's Natural History Museum, is of the opinion that what Mr. Cartwright observed was an oarfish. The oarfish is normally found in the waters north of Great Britain, but it is possible that a storm or errant current carried it to Nova Scotia waters.

Still, I wonder.

Oarfish are nature's longest fish. They have been known to reach up to fifty-five feet in length. They have a thin, snake-like appearance and usually swim in a perpendicular fashion—that is, straight up and down and moving through the water like a giant, living hockey stick.

Maybe so, but the part in me that believes in ghosts and spirits and things that go "booga-booga" in the night kind of wonders if when they say "oarfish," scientists aren't really just admitting that they've finally gone and discovered sea serpents.

A rose by any other name...

Halifax Ferry Terminal

5077 GEORGE STREET

N 44°38.98′ W 63°34.30′

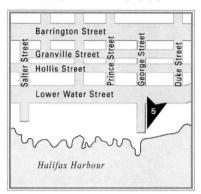

The Hanging of Peter Carteel

ARLY MAPS OF HALIFAX PROMINENTLY MARK THE LOCATION OF the city gallows and public stocks as being originally located somewhere close to the edge of Lower Water Street just handy to the Halifax Ferry Terminal, near the Celtic Cross monument that you'll see at the intersection of George Street. It is here that the ghost of Peter Carteel, the very first man ever hanged in Halifax way back in 1749, is said to walk.

I Am Gone

Back in the good old days, you could be hanged for any reason you could think of. In 1750, Thomas Munroe was hanged because he was found to be in possession of stolen clothing. A few months later, three men were sentenced to hang for the theft of a cow.

Unfair, you say? Well they never stole a cow again, did they?

In the first few weeks after Halifax was established back in 1749, Peter Carteel became the very first person to climb the Halifax hanging tree without using either his hands or his feet.

Carteel was a French sailor in an English port and he was a bit of a hothead. One morning, while onboard the *Beaufort*, Carteel fell into an argument with Boatswain's Mate Abraham Goodsides. Carteel spoke French and Goodsides spoke English. Both were having a hard time making themselves understood.

I guess Goodsides had a bad side and Peter Carteel got on it. Goodsides bridged the communication gap by slapping Carteel hard

The spirit of Peter Carteel, the first man ever hanged in Halifax, is said to haunt the ferry terminal grounds.

in the face. Carteel didn't like being slapped. He pulled out a four-inch fish knife and jammed it into Goodsides' chest, burying it to the hilt.

"I am gone," Goodsides cried out.

Goodsides fell to the deck and quickly bled out. The crowd went wild. Two other sailors were wounded in the struggle before Carteel was arrested for murder.

Elbow deep in the colonization of Halifax, Governor Edward Cornwallis appointed himself judge, appointed half a dozen stalwart citizens for a jury, and set up a makeshift courthouse in a freshly built storage building. Of course, there was a shortage of lawyers back then, but Cornwallis figured that that would smooth out the judicial process considerably.

Four witnesses were called to the stand. Three of these might have been considered biased since they were close friends and shipmates of the murdered man. The entire proceedings were interpreted for Carteel's sake by a court-appointed translator whose French was a little rusty. In the eyes of the court, Peter Carteel had been "moved and seduced by the instigation of the Devil."

On Saturday, September 2, 1749, Peter Carteel was marched to a large tree at the water's edge. They gave him a brand-new rope to wear and then they hanged him by his neck until he was dead.

From murder to execution, the entire process was accomplished in less than a week. Was this swift justice or a miscarriage? One wonders why Carteel wasn't charged with manslaughter. It could be argued that he hadn't intended to murder Goodsides, but apparently this matter wasn't even considered by the makeshift jury.

Some folks swear that a ghost still walks the area searching for justice or maybe just trying to understand what brought him to his fate. Others claim that on certain nights you can see the entire hanging tree, growing up out of the shadows of history, with the ghost of a young man swinging slowly in the dark night breeze.

Lower Water Street

LOWER WATER STREET & GEORGE STREET

N 44°38.92' W 63°34.33'

The Tale of Tomahawk

I N ADDITION TO THE GHOST OF PETER CARTEEL, THERE'S ANOTHER gallows ghost said to haunt the George Street waterfront area—the ghost of Halifax's first appointed public hangman has been seen in this vicinity. His name, according to certain history books, is Thomas Hawk, but he is otherwise known as "Tomahawk."

Tomahawk's Final Drop

George Street was the first actual street in Halifax. The early settlers cleared a road straight from the gallows at the water's edge right on up to the Grand Parade and branched out from there.

The gallows was originally nothing more than a sturdy tree, but it did the job just fine. In 1763, the tree was cut down and a proper gallows was built. The ground was rocky and slippery around the gallows at high tide, but it was in an ideal location because it could be seen from as far away as the Parade Square.

From the shoreline, the Grand Parade was nothing but a steep climb uphill—as was all of Halifax back then but—of course, a steep climb beats a fast drop any day you care to mention. And this brings us to the story of Thomas Hawk, Halifax's first official hangman.

Being a hangman can be nearly as popular a profession as being a tax collector, a dentist, or an undertaker. As a result, many hangmen wore hoods and adopted pseudonyms in order to preserve their anonymity.

Peering through the trees on George Street. It is hard to imagine that this area was once home to the main Halifax gallows.

However, back in 1750 Halifax's first official hangman was one Thomas Hawk, otherwise known as Tommy Hawk or "Tomahawk." Noted Nova Scotia author Thomas H. Raddall writes in his book *Halifax: Warden of the North* that Tommy Hawk lived in a rundown shanty alongside the northern blockhouse somewhere handy to the location of the present-day Fairview Cemetery. There, he spent his days between hangings drinking copious amounts of strong Jamaican rum. He was a loner with a dirty job and a bad reputation as a trouble-making reprobate, yet he took his task seriously.

One morning, a group of young men found the stone-cold dead body of old Tomahawk lying at the doorstep of his shanty. Perhaps he drank himself to death. Perhaps his heart did him in. Those young Halifax men didn't really care, to tell you the truth. They dragged his body to a nearby outhouse, slung a noose around his neck, and hanged him down the hole. They likely laughed about it too. Hanging the hangman was considered high old humour back in the day.

According to Raddall, Tomahawk's shanty and the outhouse where he was hanged stood just off of where Windsor Street now runs, next to the present-day Fairview Lawn Cemetery. You will read of this cemetery a little later in the collection when you come to the story of the Titanic gravesite.

Tomahawk's body hung in the latrine for seventy years and was anointed by weak-bladdered wayfarers who stopped to use the privy. His ghost was said to haunt the ruins of his shanty, and some folks claimed that his spirit still watched over the George Street gallows and greeted the customers as they dropped through to whatever lay on the other side of the gallows trap door.

Historic Properties

1869 UPPER WATER STREET

N 44°39.02' W 63°34.39'

The Privateer's Warehouse Ghost

THE GHOST OF ENOS COLLINS, AN EARLY HALIFAX BUSINESSMAN and known privateer, is said to prowl the corridors of the Historic Properties. He has been seen by more than a few employees of the local businesses. Keep an eye open and you might see him as well as he prowls through the shadows of the hallways just outside the Lower Deck tavern door.

A Shipping Venture

Enos Collins—merchant, ship owner, banker, and reputedly one of the richest men in Canada back in the early nineteenth century—earned a great deal of his working capital from privateering. In addition to privateering, Collins helped found, in 1825, the Halifax Banking Company, known nowadays as the Canadian Imperial Bank of Commerce. Collins owned several privateer vessels, including the infamous *Liverpool Packet*, which captured and looted at least thirty-three American vessels during the War of 1812.

A privateer was a government-licensed pirate who through the purchase of a letter of marque was given the privilege of seizing any enemy-owned merchant vessels and making a profit from selling the cargo or the vessel itself. Collins bankrolled privateers and made a profit storing and auctioning off seized goods in a large, ironstone warehouse that still stands down in Halifax's famous Historic Properties.

Collins's ghost is reputed to haunt the offices of the Privateer's Warehouse and the surrounding area. Employees have reported seeing a ghostly shadow moving through the hallway. Footsteps have also been heard echoing through the darkened halls, and some employees have actually refused to stay after dark. Perhaps Collins is waiting for one more shipment or hoping to strike one final deal.

Or, maybe he's just hoping to catch himself a good bargain or two at one of the local tourist shops.

Collins's Melancholy Baby

There is a little-known and quite macabre connection between Enos Collins and the famous English writer, Charles Dickens. Dickens, on his first tour of North America, arrived in Halifax Harbour in 1842. It was a cold, foggy, and dismal day, and his ship ran hard aground on a mudbank.

Nova Scotia, Dickens declared, was "dark, foggy and damp." He decided that Halifax was a "curiosity of ugly dullness." However, writers—like gold miners picking away in the unlit belly of a mine shaft, looking for the shine of gold—will salvage the brightest bit of glitter from the darkest depths of despair.

The Lower Deck was once part of the Privateer's Warehouse on the Halifax waterfront.

During his journey, Dickens overheard a story concerning a young woman who fell in love with a man and planned to marry. It seems the cad jilted her and left her standing at the altar. She went quite mad and spent the rest of her life dressed in her wedding gown, waiting in vain for her errant groom's return.

Dickens was enchanted by that story and he seized upon it, crafting Miss Haversham in his novel *Great Expectations*. Now, this wasn't that flattering an inspiration, considering that Miss Haversham is a rather pathetic, scheming character who huddled in the twisted nostalgic memories of the marriage that never happened, determined to do everything in her power to end the expectation of love for any who came into contact with her.

The truth of the matter is that the lonely, jilted bride was none other than Enos Collins's very own daughter. His daughter reportedly spent many years in a private lunatic asylum in Boston. It wasn't recorded whether or not she wore her bridal gown or if anyone thought to throw confetti upon her grave.

I wonder where her ghost walks....

The Angus L. Macdonald Bridge

HALIFAX HARBOUR

N 44°39.8' W 63°35.1'

Curses Come in Threes

L EGEND HAS IT THAT A MI'KMAQ CURSE WAS PLACED OVER THE waters of the Bedford Basin known as the Narrows, dooming any attempt to bridge those waters. There have been three bridges built across these waters. The first two attempts failed. Folks wonder just when this third attempt is going to join the first two at the bottom of Halifax Harbour; I suspect some still wonder while they're driving over the bridge if they're going to be up there over the angry Narrows water when it finally does happen.

The Legend of the Curse

Three times a bridge over these waves shall rise
built by the white man, so strong and so wise
three times shall fall like a dying breath
in storm, in silence, and last in death.
—Anonymous poem, *Halifax Herald*

Halifax Harbour is crossed by two bridges, and both of them are pretty hard to miss. The bridge closest to the harbour mouth is the Angus L. Macdonald Bridge, or the "old bridge" as some folks call it, and the bridge farther inland is known as the A. Murray MacKay Bridge, or the "new bridge." The bridge in question in this story is the Angus L. Macdonald Bridge. With an average of nearly forty thousand vehicles crossing over its nearly one-mile span daily, Macdonald Bridge is one of the busiest stretches of Halifax roadway.

After thirty-six months of hard work, over 8,000 tons of steel, nearly 430,000 rivets, and 1.4 million pounds of concrete, the bridge was opened on April 2, 1955. One wonders if the day wasn't deliberately chosen in order to avoid the curse of April Fool's Day. However, the Angus L. Macdonald Bridge was not the first harbour crossing.

And as I've said, some believe it is cursed.

The Angus L. Macdonald Bridge still stands despite the curse that is rumoured to have brought down its predecessors.

The Curse

There is an old legend that people have told for a lot of years. It's one of the first tales that I heard upon my arrival in Halifax over three decades ago and, as so often goes, the tale begins with a broken heart.

It seems that sometime back in the early eighteenth century, a lonely English sailor fell in love with a Mi'kmaq woman. Unfortunately, she was already promised to a Mi'kmaq brave — the son of a chief, or so they say. The sailor had ideas of his own as to whom that lady was promised.

The Mi'kmaq brave and his wife lived in a tent on the Dartmouth shore of the harbour. In fact, there was a small Mi'kmaq settlement along the banks of Tufts Cove, known then as Turtle Cove, which is right about where those three candy-cane-striped smokestacks poke out from beyond the A. Murray MacKay Bridge. The settlement's location has been dated back to the early 1700s; however, it was completely destroyed in the Halifax Explosion of 1917.

The sailor smooth-talked his way into the Mi'kmaq woman's heart and she promised to run away with him. I've always had the feeling that the sailor didn't really care all that much for her. He was nothing more than a trifler; nevertheless, by the light of a hunter's moon she stole away with him from her tent.

The Mi'kmaq warrior caught them in the act and chased them to the shore. Just as the lovers were climbing into a dory that the sailor had waiting for them, the warrior, armed with a sharp hatchet, sprang out of the darkness.

Now some say the Mi'kmaq brave cut down his wife by mistake while others say she threw herself in the path of the blade to protect her English lover. In any case, the hatchet split her heart in two and her blood stained the rocks of the shore where she fell.

In the excitement the sailor managed to row away. The heartbroken warrior threw his bloodstained hatchet out into the water and dove in trying to catch the sailor. Unfortunately, the waters were too rough for the warrior to overtake the skillfully rowing sailor. Before he had swum more than a hundred yards from the shore, he sank beneath the waves. Perhaps the current was too strong for him or maybe in despair and grief he simply gave up the ghost.

His father, a chief of the Mi'kmaq, walked the shores in search of his son. When he found no trace of the body, the old chief howled his grief and cast a soulful curse out over the Narrows water.

"First in a storm, second in silence, and third in death," he said in Mi'kmaq, of course, and it sounded a lot different ringing out over those lonesome, fog-ridden waters. He chanted the incantation until his heart broke in two and he lay upon the hard rocky shore of Halifax Harbour and joined his son in whatever world might wait beyond.

The Narrows as it looks from the Angus L. Macdonald Bridge. The Narrows is said to be the watery grave of the son of a Mi'kmaq chief.

First in Storm

The first bridge spanning the width of Halifax Harbour was built in 1884 by the Intercolonial Railway. It was a flimsy creation built of pine with water-resistant hemlock pilings driven down into supporting bases of timber-framed rock. Each supporting base contained in excess of twenty tons of heaped boulders.

The bridge itself was a long, fish-hooked railroad trestle divided in the middle by an iron swing-bridge which could swivel open in order to allow ships to pass through between the outer Halifax Harbour and the inner Bedford Basin.

That worked for a while; however, a storm that arrived one Monday morning on September 7, 1891, had disastrous consequences on the bridge. Following a steady rainfall and some mild weather, the wind backed around and brewed up into what was alternately described as a cyclone, a gale, and a baby hurricane. According to an article in the September 8th issue of the *Acadian Recorder*, the storm was pretty fierce. Sheets of rain slashed down along with a raging wind that reached forty miles an hour at least.

The trees bowed to the dirt, the sky inked over, and at midnight nearly 1,000 of the 1,500-yard bridge was ripped from its supporting ballast bases, leaving nothing but the shards of a few broken timbers that poked up from beneath the rolling harbour waves.

The damage was estimated at over fifty thousand dollars, which was a considerable sum back in the late nineteenth century. Railcars were marooned in Dartmouth and harbour traffic was obstructed for weeks afterwards by the tangled snarl of leftover debris.

First in storm, indeed.

Second in Silence

The bridge was hastily rebuilt upon the original mooring and was even flimsier than before. On the morning of July 24, 1893, following the passage of a heavily laden coal train, the larger half of the bridge simply floated away and slowly tipped over. When they had reattached the supporting trestles to the boulder ballast bases, they had attempted to drive the timber down into the boulders. However, because the ballast had long settled, the timber trestles jammed in a little and then snapped unnoticed.

That morning, an uncommonly heavy tide raised the trestles up from their supporting foundation and floated the whole structure away. The greater part of the Narrows Bridge was sunken in the belly of the Bedford Basin. Further examination proved that the shoddy construction was further hindered by the fact that the trestles were worm-eaten, almost through, between the high-water and the low-water marks.

Again, there were thirty-four freight, box, and coal cars stranded on the Dartmouth side. Thankful that at least no lives had been lost in the unexpected catastrophe, the powers-that-be decided that the bridge should never be rebuilt.

Second, in silence.

That's two down if you're keeping count.

Thwarting the Curse

In 1943, Mayor Leonard Isnor of Dartmouth urged the Royal Commission on Post-War Planning to recommend that a bridge be constructed across Halifax Harbour after the war ended. The recommendation was accepted on November 16, 1945 — five months after the war ended.

Angus L. Macdonald, then the premier of Nova Scotia, hired bridge engineer Philip L. Pratley to investigate the feasibility of such a structure. By 1955, one year following the death of Angus L. Macdonald, the bridge was built and named after the deceased premier.

However, someone must have remembered the story of the curse and decided that all bets must be covered. Mi'kmaq elders were consulted and a one-hundred-year-old Mi'kmaq holy woman prayed and fasted and communed with the ancient spirits in an attempt to decide upon the manner in which the curse could be lifted.

When the bridge opened, a small band of Mi'kmaq performed a ceremony in which self-proclaimed "Chief of Friendship" James Paul from Indian Brook danced across the bridge as his companions sang and chanted with him. However, when asked afterwards about the actual circumstances behind the bridge curse, James Paul admitted that he'd never heard of such a curse.

Whether or not the bridge is actually cursed, I can tell you that you will be able to sense all manner of ill feelings in the wind and hear an awful lot of cursing — along with the racket of car horns — as scores of motorists line up on the Macdonald Bridge on any given rush-hour morning.

I recommend earplugs if you're the least bit sensitive.

Little Dutch Church

GERRISH STREET & BRUNSWICK STREET

N 44°39.34' W 63°35.13'

Creeping through the Crypt

I N THE MID-1990S, A TEAM OF ARCHAEOLOGISTS UNCOVERED several unmarked mass graves beneath this tiny church. Over two-dozen skeletons were unearthed in this macabre little story.

The History of the Church

The original band of future Haligonians who followed Cornwallis onto the shore and helped found the city of Halifax was definitely a fairly irregular bunch. They had been promised money and land and a year's worth of provisions and free transportation to the land of milk and honey. In return they were expected to buckle down and build a city.

However, not a lot of them were all that keen on that whole buckling-down notion. Some of them preferred to sit in the shade of an oak tree rather than go to the trouble of cutting it down. Others vanished in the first month or two of settlement, making their way down to Boston where the living promised to be easier.

Discouraged with the performance of his English settlers, Cornwallis looked for more reliable help elsewhere. In 1750, he requested that the British Lords of Trade should send a tougher lot of settlers. Cornwallis had German farmers in mind. What Cornwallis wanted was exactly what Cornwallis got. Between 1750 and 1752, nearly three thousand German, French, and Swiss settlers arrived in Halifax. The majority of these European families settled in the northern side of the city and in 1756 they built their own church.

The settlers moved a house directly onto a portion of the burial ground at the corner of Brunswick and Gerrish streets where the church now stands. The Church was known as the Little Dutch Church—the word "Dutch" being a bastardization of the German word *Deutsche*, which is how the predominantly German population referred to themselves and their church.

By 1758, the tiny church, some twenty by forty feet in dimension, was finished inside at the expense of one Otto William Schwartz, an ancestor of the famous Schwartz spice family. Later, in 1842, a bell was salvaged from the ruins of a fallen Louisbourg and served to ring the congregation into worship.

The little church served its community for several decades. However, by the year 1800 the congregation had outgrown the tiny church. In 1800 a larger facility was constructed a block to the south; it was a round church built in the style dictated by the "amateur architecture" of His Royal Highness Prince Edward.

St. George's Round Church on Brunswick Street

The larger church is known as St. George's Round Church and it too has its own miraculous story. In June 1994, three young boys broke into the church and started a fire. A significant portion of the church was burned to the ground.

Thanks to the fundraising efforts of the congregation, St. George's Round Church was raised up like a phoenix from out of the ashes and is in service to this day.

A Dreadful Discovery

While St. George's Round Church was being reconstructed, the Little Dutch Church was used as a stopgap place of worship. In order to use the old facilities, the Little Dutch Church's crumbling foundations needed to be repaired. Under the legal provisions of the Nova Scotia Special Places Protection Act (1991), the historic nature of the place necessitated archaeological assessment prior to any such work.

It was then that a macabre discovery was made by a team of St. Mary's University archaeologists. In addition to the expected crypts that contained the remains of several notable citizens, including the body of old Otto Schwartz, there was a secondary layer and a strange mass grave composed of at least ten bodies, heaped up two or three deep.

The remains were removed to the university's physical anthropology laboratory and analyzed. After much study it was decided that these skeletons were what was left from the casualties of a typhus outbreak on one of the first shiploads of German settlers.

The story did not end there.

By June 1998, the investigating crew discovered a second mass grave beneath the church. This burial site was considerably cruder than the first and contained the jumbled skeletons of at least fourteen more individuals. The remains were again studied and this time the investigators were surprised to discover that of the fourteen bodies found, six were of black descent and one was Mi'kmaq.

It seems that an earlier repair job of the church, due to some roadwork on nearby Brunswick Street, led to the inadvertent excavation of fourteen gravesites back in 1896. The workers hastily threw the bones back into a few handy, wooden tubs and reburied them in a mass grave.

The story ended in 1998 when the remains of all the uncovered dead of the Little Dutch Church were sorted and casketed and reburied. The singing of a German hymn and the performance of a Mi'kmaq sweetgrass ceremony hopefully ensured that the twice-desecrated dead will finally rest in peace.

There are folks who claim that the spirits of these dead still walk the graveyard that surrounds this tiny church. Shapes and figures have been seen moving through the tombstones. As of yet, no one has reported an actual face-to-face encounter, but there are a lot of restless spirits out there.

In August 1999, the Little Dutch (*Deutsche*) Church was officially commemorated and declared a site of national historic significance. Perhaps now those restless spirits will finally find their much-needed peace.

Halifax Alehouse

1717 BRUNSWICK STREET

N 44°38.80' W 63°34.598'

The Brunswick Street Flutist

ACCORDING TO A VERY OLD LEGEND, THE GHOST OF A YOUNG orphan boy walks down Brunswick Street near the Halifax Alehouse on foggy, moonless nights, playing a soft, sad refrain on an old tin whistle. This is a ghost story from nineteenth-century Halifax that not a lot of local storytellers recollect. In fact, I first came across the tale of the Brunswick Street flutist in Clary Croft's entertaining 2004 collection *Nova Scotia Moments*.

Just Give a Listen

Is that the sound of the wind whistling?

Brunswick Street began back in the eighteenth century with the building of the Little Dutch Church, the first Lutheran Church in Canada. However, it soon grew into a rowdy road known as Barracks Street, although most folks just referred to it as "Knock-'Em-Down Street."

In the five short city blocks that it occupied, there were army bar-

The Halifax Alehouse

racks at each end, and stretched in between were more brothels and booze halls than you could shake a billy club at. It was a street that you didn't want to be caught dead on, and if a body wasn't careful, it might very well live up to that grim little prophecy. Following numerous complaints, the street was renamed South Brunswick Street in the 1870s in hope that the new name would somehow remedy the street's bad reputation.

Stopping for a Smoke

There are more than a few stories to be found around Brunswick Street and at least a couple of them involve ghosts.

According to the December 16, 1867, issue of the *Acadian Recorder*, a ghost of approximately twelve to sixteen feet in height was seen several times walking down from Citadel Hill and along Brunswick Street. He was dressed in a uniform of the British army and was seen pausing to lean down over a lamppost to light his pipe. A local Halifax police officer reportedly chased the giant apparition who either vanished into or through a Brunswick Street window, perhaps in search of a talent scout from the nineteenth-century version of the NBA.

Brunswick Street from the side of Citadel Hill

Whistling Another Tune

It was around that same time that the residents of Brunswick Street began telling a story about a young orphan boy who eked out a miserable living playing a tin flute for passersby. He would sit outside the taverns, tootling his tin flute, hoping the sound of his music was enough to coax a penny or two from a drunkard's pocket.

Then one night, a tavern keeper wondered where the boy had gone. He hadn't been seen in several weeks, yet folks continued to hear the sound of his wee tin flute eerily piping on dark, foggy nights.

A group of soldiers searched the area where the music seemed the loudest and they found the bones of a small boy in a nearby abandoned cellar. Whether the boy had been murdered for the pitiful bit of money he'd earned or he'd just crawled in there one night and passed away, no one could say. However, after they buried the boy in the Poor House Cemetery with his tin flute, the music was no longer heard.

Still, give a listen when you walk Brunswick Street by night and see if you can hear the thin, eerie strains of the Brunswick Street flutist.

I dare you to try whistling along.

Halifax Citadel

N 44°38.8' W 63°34.8'

The Sergeant in the Well

T HE ONE-ARMED GHOST OF A SERGEANT WHO DROWNED UNDER suspicious circumstances in a well during a fire in the Citadel barracks is said to haunt the courtyard and has been seen standing stiffly at attention by the unused well in which he reportedly perished. The well can be found on the north end of the inner Citadel, behind a closed and locked door in Casemate 18. Just ask one of the Citadel staff members to point out Casement 18 and you'll have a better idea of where to look.

Not an Angry Shot

There are a lot of ghost stories found in our next site—the Halifax Citadel. I'll retell one of them, but I recommend that you tour the facilities on one of their regular ghost walks. I guarantee you will hear a lot more stories from the tour guides than I have time or room enough to tell. But this one is definitely my favourite.

Every noon, without fail, it is a popular pastime for those locals working downtown to watch for the tourists who duck and cover when the noontime gun goes off at Citadel Hill.

Of course, the truth is there isn't anything to be frightened of. There actually hasn't been a shot fired in anger at the Citadel in over 250 years unless you count the 1868 incident when a salute was fired in honour of Canada's first birthday, and an accidental cannon discharge killed two soldiers and wounded several others.

A guard stands ready at the entrance to the Halifax Citadel.

Life in the Citadel was hard. A soldier earned a shilling a day—that's about twelve cents, not counting the deductions for food and uniforms and supplies. Barracks were cold, damp, and crowded. Discipline was rigidly enforced. If you were found to be a troublemaker, the initials *BC* for "Bad Character" were branded onto your chest.

Desertion might earn you a capital *D* if you were lucky. You could be hanged or flogged or thrown into the stocks or dragged behind Citadel Hill to what they now call the Garrison Grounds, where you would be shot and buried.

Even if you behaved, life was rough. A communal urine tub was used as an evening toilet. In the morning, the urine-filled tub was rinsed out and filled with water so the men could wash their faces and hands.

Cleanliness is next to godliness, or so they say.

Fire in the Hole

In 1850, a colour-sergeant by the name of O'Reilly had a reputation of being a bit of a brute and a bully. For those who don't know, the colour-sergeant was responsible for guarding the regimental flags in battle. You had to be tough to handle that job. On the battlefield back then, the regimental colours drew an awful lot of unwanted attention.

O'Reilly made a hobby out of terrorizing a young private named Billy. O'Reilly beat Billy any chance he got; he assigned him extra duties and cursed him out daily.

"Hard work never hurt a lad," O'Reilly scornfully said. "It'll build his character."

Bullying is bound to bring comeuppance. O'Reilly met his retribution when a fire broke out at three in the morning in the portion of the North Barracks where the officers of the Eighty-eighth Regiment were quartered. The barracks were constructed out of a resinous pine lumber, and within minutes the flames were raging uncontrollably and the entire structure was consumed.

In all the confusion no one quite noticed when Sergeant O'Reilly quietly disappeared. However, on the next morning when the roll call was taken, O'Reilly and Billy were nowhere to be seen. Some thought they were lost in the fire. Others believed the two soldiers deserted in the confusion. Nobody was surprised by either theory. A soldier's life was hard and desertion was never an unexpected event.

An Unexpected Discovery

In the winter of 1851, months later, a soldier was sent to draw water from the well at Casement 18. The windlass through which the well rope turned was jammed. It took three soldiers to free the jam. Once the bucket was drawn out of the well, the men were horrified to see what was tangled in the rope.

They found a severed human arm, rotten and putrid from soaking so long in the water. The dirty white shoulder bone was still attached and was clad in the tatters of a bright red British uniform adorned with the crossed swords and flag of a colour-sergeant's insignia.

What had happened?

At first it was thought that O'Reilly had gone to fetch water to fight the fire and had fallen into the well. Then time and the natural putre-fying qualities of standing water worked their ooey-gooey magic.

However, when they dragged the rest of O'Reilly's carcass out of the well, they found a bullet hole in his back. He had been murdered in cold blood and his body tipped into the well. Billy shot O'Reilly and deserted.

For years afterward, O'Reilly's ghost has been seen standing stiffly at attention in the courtyard by the well. Some claim that he is armless, although I imagine he died with his arm intact. Others claim that he carries his missing arm with him. I rather like that image. I can picture the ghostly sergeant standing with his arm propped over his shoulder like a rifle.

Attention!

Present arm!

Citadel Hill

FORT GEORGE

N 44°38.8' W 63°34.8'

The George's Island Tunnels of Mystery

OW THAT I HAVE YOU FOLKS STANDING HERE AT CITADEL HILL, I want you to take a good look around you. All of those streets that lead from the Citadel down to the shore of the harbour are riddled with mysterious tunnels. Sackville Street, Prince Street, George Street, and Duke Street—each of them hides a tunnel that leads down towards the waterfront.

What are the tunnels there for? No one really knows for sure, but the entire downtown core is honeycombed with these mysterious brick-lined tunnels. Some believe the tunnels were a secret means of reinforcing or retreating from the Citadel during a time of siege. Others claim the tunnels are nothing but old-fashioned sewers.

Maybe Really Big Gophers?

When the first settlers settled Halifax back in 1749, one of their first priorities was the building of a large wooden stockade linked with five strategically placed wooden blockhouses. One of these blockhouses, erected atop the naturally forming drumlin that looked down over Halifax Harbour, could be considered the basis for the Halifax Citadel that we know today.

It must have been the first thing those settlers noticed, standing there wet and cold from their journey, on that rocky strip of a beach and looking up one hell of a slope.

"We're going to build there?" somebody was sure to have asked.

"We'll build here," some hairy-legged man in a kilt was bound to have answered. "Here, where it's steepest."

The second Citadel was an even larger blockhouse surrounded by a series of irregular earthworks. There didn't seem to be much forethought behind its design. It was constructed around the time of the American Revolution. The governing British were nervous at the thought of all of those uppity Colonialists revolting down south and were perhaps concerned about us uppity Nova Scotia folk getting ideas of independence.

It was Prince Edward who raised the third Citadel around the time of the French Revolution. Or rather, he lowered it first. In order to create a proper foundation for the mighty fortress he envisioned, Prince Edward had the top of Citadel Hill lowered by about forty feet. It was a massive undertaking, but Edward felt it necessary to allow for a proper field of fire. He ordered that the hill be levelled, and then constructed a third Citadel, naming it Fort George after the king.

In 1825, the Duke of Wellington commissioned an intensive study on the effectiveness of this third Citadel. What was there wasn't enough to handle the demands of Napoleonic warfare. Something had to be done. By 1853 the fort, at nearly double the predicted expense and time, was as complete as it would ever be.

The Tunnels

In 1919, James Gowen of the city engineers department discovered a stone-walled tunnel leading down from the top of George Street while he was supervising a road-paving crew. The tunnel, measuring approximately five feet high by three feet wide, was a snug fit for most men, but at a crouch it was quite accessible.

"This was no ordinary sewer," Gowen said. "Its construction and the direction led us to believe it was a passage. It had a wooden floor and well-built sides. It's my opinion it was an escape tunnel. It was never used for a sanitary sewer."

In 1973, the same tunnel was rediscovered at the harbour-end of George Street when a cave-in occurred during another round of roadwork. A city inspector entered the tunnel and followed it for as long as he had time for. He discovered there were branch tunnels forking off from the main run. These branch tunnels led to the basements of many old Victorian buildings including the old post office, which is the site of the current-day Art Gallery of Nova Scotia. One wonders why an expedition wasn't allowed to further explore the tunnel and seek out its terminus. It was sealed up and paved over. They had deadlines to keep, after all.

A second tunnel, running beneath Duke Street just outside the present-day Metro Centre, was discovered in 1938. Douglas Fraser, a professional engineer, reported he had entered a roomy, stone-walled tunnel that measured approximately six feet wide by eight feet high; it was definitely man-sized. The tunnel led down towards the harbour, but it was sealed up and seemingly forgotten. In 1977, the same tunnel was opened at the corner of Duke and Granville streets just across from the Nova Scotia College of Art and Design.

Back in 1958, a smaller tunnel was found at the corner of Brunswick and Buckingham. Don't look for Buckingham Street on the Halifax map. Scotia Square Mall now covers what used to be Buckingham Street as well as several smaller streets and lanes. At the time, it was theorized that this small tunnel led to an even larger tunnel that passed beneath Buckingham Street.

In the late summer of 1976, a Nova Scotia Power crew, busily erecting a utility pole close to the corner of Grafton and Prince streets, broke straight down through the stone roof of what the crew described as "a well-constructed narrow passageway."

The clock tower off Brunswick Street may be on top of a secret tunnel running out from the Citadel.

This time the media was alerted. The *Halifax Herald* sent journalist Barbara Hinds and photographer Lee Wamboldt to investigate. The two followed the smaller tunnel into a larger tunnel that passed beneath Prince Street and also headed from the Citadel down to the harbour. This tunnel had a six-foot-high arched stone roof and alcoves carved at intervals along its length where perhaps candles, lanterns, or torches once stood. It had a crypt-like appearance and a sturdily-crafted wooden floor.

An Escape Tunnel?

Ever since that first tunnel was uncovered, folks have theorized that there must be some sort of an "escape tunnel" running from Fort George to George's Island. The official story circulated by the Canadian army back in 1919 was that these tunnels were nothing more than sewer pipes.

Yet that doesn't explain the "honey wagons" that rolled up Citadel Hill to Fort George to carry away the septic waste several times a week. Nor did it explain the downtown streets, which were often described as "open-air sewers." In fact, the City of Halifax didn't even install its first public urinal until 1888.

Finally, a team of independent researchers in the late 1970s ran a chemical analysis of splinters taken from the wood flooring of the George Street tunnel. No biological trace of human waste was found in the pieces of wood they studied. That washed the sewer theory straight down the drain.

John William Cameron's Secret

John William Cameron was a nineteenth-century master mason who was reputedly contracted in the late 1860s by the Royal Army to take on a top secret Halifax project. Both he and his crew were sworn to secrecy. The project took several years to complete. Once it was finished, Cameron was dismissed and the workers went their separate ways.

However, word leaked out. Rumours of an escape route from the Citadel to George's Island began to circulate amongst the general populace. The authorities kept denying the story, claiming that any tunnels beneath Halifax were nothing more than a series of brick sewers.

John William Cameron passed away in 1927 at the age of eighty-six without letting the secret slip.

A Mystery to This Very Day

So is there an escape tunnel?

I believe there's some truth to this rumour. Every fortress needed a few exits from which to sortie against the enemy, sneak out messages, or reinforce its position.

George's Island has always served as a natural fortress and landing point. This is why the unfortunate Duc d'Anville chose this spot to land and set up camp in 1746. This is why Cornwallis chose to land here three years later and set up the initial British home base. The island is a natural fortress, fairly inaccessible short of a determined amphibious assault. I believe it is conceivable that the military mind might have decided that a secret reinforcement of the Citadel, to protect it if under siege, might best be accomplished by sea.

Furthermore, a reconstruction project at Fort Charlotte on George's Island did include the construction of a maze of underground tunnels and passages. However, the sheer engineering of such a tunnel, nearly half a mile long and passing underneath Halifax Harbour, seems unbelievable. In any case, the tunnels are real and do exist. Downtown Halifax is fairly riddled with them.

It is a fascinating and dark mystery even to this very day. Perhaps someday somebody will finally get to the bottom of all this.

Halifax City Hall

1841 ARGYLE STREET

N 44°38.89' W 63°34.52'

Where Time Stands Still

HIGH ATOP THE SEVEN-STOREY TOWER OF HALIFAX CITY HALL IS A clock with faces on the north and south sides. The northern face that looks down onto Duke Street is fixed at four minutes past nine as a silent reminder commemorating the two thousand victims of the Halifax Explosion of 1917.

Time Stands Still

If you stand on the front steps of Scotia Square Mall at the corner of Duke Street and Barrington Street and stare across Duke Street, you are staring at the rear view of Halifax City Hall. The site was originally the home of Dalhousie University, and for years the City of Halifax and Dalhousie University arm wrestled over who would own the Grand Parade. In the end, the city made Dalhousie University an offer it could not refuse. Dalhousie moved to its current location and the old university was knocked down to facilitate the construction of the brand-new City Hall.

City Hall also served double duty as a jailhouse and a magistrate's court until 1890.

On December 6, 1917, the explosive-laden French cargo ship *Mont*

Halifax City Hall's Duke Street clock commemorates the exact moment of the Halifax Explosion of 1917.

Blanc inadvertently collided with the Norwegian freighter *Imo* resulting in one of the world's largest man-made conventional explosions to date—the Halifax Explosion. The explosion obliterated a good part of the city, creating a small tsunami and a pressure wave of air current that rattled windows as far away as Prince Edward Island.

Halifax's mayor was out of town at the time, but Deputy Mayor Henry Colwell took charge as best as he could. Colwell sent out a message to Moncton that went as follows:

"For God's sake send out additional messages to the different towns of Nova Scotia and New Brunswick asking for further relief."

He signed it—"Mayor of Halifax."

The City Hall clock was stopped by the force of the explosion at precisely four minutes past nine o'clock. Since then, a new clock was installed; however, you can only tell the true time while staring up from the Grand Parade, which sits between City Hall and St. Paul's Church, bounded by Duke and Prince streets and Barrington and Argyle streets. The face of the clock that overlooks Duke Street has been fixed at four minutes past nine o'clock to commemorate the monumental explosion.

The Five Fishermen

1740 ARGYLE STREET

N 44°38.86' W 63°34.507'

Terror in the Kitchen

THE GHOSTLY HAPPENINGS THAT GO ON INSIDE HALIFAX'S FAVOU-rite seafood restaurant, the Five Fishermen, are known interna-tionally. A crew from the Discovery Channel filmed an episode about the restaurant for their popular paranormal television series *Creepy Canada*. The spirits have been written about in newspapers and magazines across the Maritimes.

The ghost has called out staff member's names, flashed the lights, dropped dishes, and played the occasional prank. I don't know about you, but the whole thing sounds an awful lot like some waiters I know.

What's on the Menu

There are some locations in Nova Scotia that are haunted beyond a shadow of a doubt. Halifax's restaurant with a reputation for ghosts would have to be the Five Fishermen. Now, I've eaten there and in their little brother restaurant below—Little Fish—and I can tell you that it's the home of good dining and Halifax's best mussels.

However, the Five Fishermen is also the home of a haunt.

The building was built back in 1817 and was home to the First National School. Following that, Anna Leonowens (more famously known as Anna, the tutor of the King of Siam, and immortalized in *The King and I*) bought the building and opened the Halifax Victorian School of Art which eventually grew up to become the Nova Scotia College of Art and Design.

Our story begins with the third business to set up in the old building. This was Snow and Sons Mortuary—the first resting place for both the dead of the *Titanic* in 1912 and the bodies recovered from the Halifax Explosion of 1917. Some folks will tell you that the current kitchen was

A popular restaurant today, the Five Fishermen on Argyle Street has a spooky past dating back to 1817.

once the processing room for the cadavers; however, I haven't been able to find a floor plan of the original mortuary to verify such a claim. I expect the claim is nothing more than an urban legend.

Nevertheless, the past of the Five Fishermen is filled with a gamut of paranormal activity. Doors are slammed, lights are turned on and off unexpectedly, silverware is thrown through the air, and voices are heard arguing in the night. Shapes and shadows and figures are seen stealing through the halls.

One of the staff found a broken ashtray on the floor of an otherwise unoccupied room. After stooping to clean up the mess, he stood back up and spotted the reflection of an old man with long, silver-grey hair and a floor-length black cloak. The old man turned and walked away and the staff member swore that the old man had walked away straight through the wall mirror.

Another night, an assistant manager by the name of Leonard Currie was talking on the telephone when he noticed the same elderly man, or at least an elderly man who matched the description.

"I'll be right with you," Leonard called out, but when he hung up the phone the apparition had somehow vanished.

The creepy part of this story is that Currie claims that he wasn't aware of the restaurant's eerie history at the time that he saw the old man waiting for him. As far as he knew, there was nothing spooky about the Five Fishermen at all.

There have also been sightings of two strange-looking women dressed in Victorian garb who walk up the stairs and then vanish. Sometimes the sound of conversation is heard in the empty rooms and inexplicable cold chills run up and down customers as if a wind were blowing from somewhere cold.

Since then, the restaurant has been investigated by paranormal investigators, television crews, psychics, and newspaper reporters. The food is still good and it is one of Halifax's most popular restaurants, so the haunts aren't hurting business one little bit.

St. Paul's Church

1749 ARGYLE STREET

N 44°38.86' W 63°34.48'

A Window into the Unknown

MUCH LIKE THE HALIFAX CITY HALL CLOCK, THE TERRIBLE Halifax Explosion of December 6, 1917, is memorialized here in St. Paul's Church in what is known as the "Explosion Window." The apparent profile that can be seen in the broken glass of this window is said to resemble that of an assistant who worked here at St. Paul's in the past.

Looking through the Window

One of the earliest official structures to be raised in the city of Halifax, St. Paul's Church is the oldest Protestant church in Canada. Erected in 1750 from timbers shipped up from Boston, Massachusetts, the church has been serving parishioners and the public alike for over 250 years.

Through the years, St. Paul's Church gave services in both English and Mi'kmaq. The Royal Pew is situated here, reserved for the sole use of Her Majesty the Queen of England or an appointed royal representative.

The church is a standing archive of Nova Scotia history, with more memorial tablets hung upon the wall than any other religious building in North America. A pictorial display of the church's history further adds to the experience. There are also crypts hidden beneath the church where twenty of Halifax's early citizens are buried.

St. Paul's Church can be found on Argyle Street, not far from City Hall.

The church's organ is reputed to have been purchased from the plunder of a Spanish privateer back in 1765. It is also said that one of the church's windows, visible from the sidewalk, eerily memorializes the Halifax Explosion of December 6, 1917.

The window in question can be seen from Argyle Street. It is the third from the left on the upper level of windows. The window was broken during the explosion. Church elders claimed at the time that the profile of broken glass bore an uncanny likeness to the Reverend Jean-Baptiste Moreau, an assistant serving at St. Paul's from 1750 to 1753.

However, on the ghost walks I have attended, the tour guides tell a somewhat more lurid story. They say that at the time of the explosion, a young organist was playing the organ. Either the concussion of the blast or a shard of stained glass, depending on who is telling the story, decapitated the young organist and blasted his head straight through the Explosion Window. The window has reportedly been replaced at least three times and every time, the face has reappeared.

Besides the Explosion Window, there is a windowsill embedded in the wall over the memorial doors in the entrance way that some storytellers claim is a chunk blasted out of the *Imo*. However, when I spoke with the official church guide on tour duty through most of the summer, he told me that the *Imo* part of the legend was nothing more than urban mythology. The fact is the windowsill was a chunk blasted off from a neighbouring building. It smashed through a window and drove into the wall like a hard-flung javelin.

This window of St. Paul's Church still bears a spooky silhouette long after it was broken in the Halifax Explosion.

Imo or not, the windowsill remnant is a pretty impressive sight. The windowsill remnant has been left there for much the same reason as the Explosion Window. When you enter the church, you can see the windowsill remnant directly overhead, high up beside the top of the left balcony staircase.

Immediately following the explosion, the vestry was used as a makeshift emergency hospital and the bodies of hundreds of victims were laid in tiers around the walls. It was also St. Paul's Church that held the city's first church service on the Sunday following the explosion.

So between the memory of those interred in the crypts beneath the church and the anguish and suffering of the blast victims (the hapless and headless young organist included), I would wager that St. Paul's Church could certainly boast its fair share of ghosts.

The Halifax Club
1682 HOLLIS STREET
N 44°38.84' W 63°34.36'

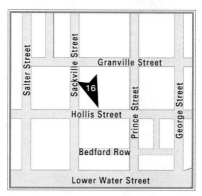

A Cold Heart and Cold Stairs

T HE HALIFAX CLUB, A LONG-ESTABLISHED LOCALE FOR HALIFAX society, is haunted by the spirit of a member who found himself in the wrong bed at the wrong time. His spirit is said to restlessly prowl the club at odd hours smoking a pipe and doing his level best to avoid going back home to face the final consequences.

A Hangout for High Society

Like the song says, "sometimes you want to go where everybody knows your name." Since 1862, the Halifax Club has been providing just that service for the staunch old nabobs in our city. It was, back then, a place for bachelors and husbands alike to congregate and just chill out. You could chow down in style, play a few hands of cards, and hang with your homeboys. That's just what the gentlemen of Halifax society would do with their leisure time back in the nineteenth century.

The front doors of the Halifax Club on Hollis Street still give the air of a private venue.

Roll Call

Mathers Byles Almon Sr., Robie Uniacke, James C. Cogswell, William Cunard—the founding members' names read like a MapQuest of Halifax. These men were a cross-section of Halifax's power structure—representing factions of the financial, political, and military establishments. The contract for constructing the Halifax Club was given to George Laing, a local builder responsible for the Sebastopol Monument in St. Paul's Cemetery and the courthouse on Spring Garden Road. Laing proved more than worthy of the task, constructing the Halifax Club in Italian Renaissance style with a heavy reliance on the adornment of a series of Doric and Ionic pillars.

The club thrived over its first decades—building a membership of what they decided was Halifax's elite. Few resigned—mostly over petty squabbles. Occasionally some gentleman would need to be reminded to pay his bill. Propriety and the reputation of its membership were given the utmost priority.

The Inevitable Scandal

In nineteenth-century Halifax, social decorum and dignity counted for much. Nevertheless, scandal occasionally kicked in the door of the Halifax Club and put its big, muddy feet smack-dab upon the tea table.

In 1870, the house steward, James Forman, was discovered dipping into the club's funds. The house steward was a position of some modest power. He lived in the club and had complete custody of the liquor cellar, the china and cutlery, the furniture, and the provisions of the club. He supervised the cook, housekeeper, servants, and the housekeeping account. When the active committee discovered that Forman had been helping himself to some of the housekeeping money, they demanded that he make good on the missing funds after which he would be allowed to quietly resign. However, Forman had other ideas.

He broke into a club meeting, screaming and babbling curses, and stabbed himself repeatedly with a carving knife before jumping out one of the second-storey windows. Forman may have botched his embezzlement career, but he was doing marvellous work in the realm of self-destruction.

Thomas Raddall describes the incident in his book *Halifax: Warden of the North* as follows: "No less startling in its way was a rude disturbance some months later in the dim recesses of the Halifax Club where the steward, yielding to an impulse that must have assailed him many times before, brought the members out of their chairs by stabbing himself repeatedly with a knife and jumping out of a window. The wretched man died; but fortunately the club recovered."

Yes, fortunately indeed. It is good to have one's priorities straight.

A Body on the Stairs

Like any of the old institutions of Halifax, the club has its very own ghost and a story to go with it.

The facts of the case are strongly based on hearsay and recollection, but the story has been told around Halifax for an awful lot of years. It seems one of the lesser-known members of the club was unlucky enough to suffer heart failure while he was indulging in a few bedroom antics with a lady of the evening in a brothel a street over.

The lady was a favourite of club members, and the last thing she desired was a scandal that would ruin her already tawdry reputation, and worse yet, alienate her with the members of the Halifax Club. Some of those members were her best customers.

She was, above all else, a practical lady.

Thinking quickly, she called the house steward who assembled an emergency task force of club members and trusted servants. They stumbled and stole over to her place of business and picked up the body of the dearly departed and carried it back to the Halifax Club. They undoubtedly made quite a sight—a caravan of nervous servants and drunken gentlemen—and I'm certain they dropped the poor soul more than a few times.

Ah well, he probably wasn't feeling any pain in the first place, and he certainly wasn't feeling anything by the time they got to lugging what was left of him. They left his body on the front steps of the club and then stepped over him as they made their way back home. In the morning when the body was found, the local papers made a great deal out of the fact that the old gentleman had died so close to the club he had loved so dearly.

Since then, various members of the club swear that they have smelled his pipe tobacco and heard his heavy footsteps especially late at night. One wonders if he's still just looking for the lady he left behind.

Or, perhaps he's just looking to pay his last bar bill.

Neptune Theatre

1593 ARGYLE STREET

N 44°38.75' W 63°34.43'

The Undying Ham

NEPTUNE THEATRE HAS BEEN HOME TO MANY A PERFORMANCE but none more chilling than the antics of the strange spirit that is said by some to haunt its stage. This ghostly player reportedly takes his bows any chance he can get and does his level best to steal the thunder of the actors and win himself another standing ovation.

A Curtain Call from Beyond the Grave

Standing squarely on the southeast corner of Argyle and Sackville streets, this site has been the home of theatrical entertainment since as far back as 1915 when the Strand Theatre graduated from vaudeville to dramatic entertainment.

By 1928, the Strand had given way to the Odeon movie theatre. However, demand for live drama was growing. In 1962, Colonel Sidney Oland of Oland Brewery provided the necessary financial backing to purchase the Odeon, and with the help of some judicious fundraising the Neptune was born. Over the late 1980s, work began on rebuilding the sadly ailing structure, and by September 1997 the new Neptune, as you see it now, opened with a presentation of Bernard Shaw's *Major Barbara*.

The Neptune Theatre adds culture to the corner of Argyle and Sackville.

The Neptune has long been haunted by a spirit the staff members affectionately refer to as "Syd the Ham." Footsteps have been heard at night and chains have actually been rattled. Most believe that Syd is an old vaudeville actor who fell from the grid—the framework of steel or wooden beams above the stage, used to support lighting and the occasional piece of flying scenery.

"He was up there fixing a light," the stage manager said. "He shouldn't have been up there but that was 'Syd the Ham' for you. He never was much good at doing what he was told."

The spirit of Syd has been seen over the years during various performances. He has become a bit of a lucky charm for the Neptune. Actors, always a superstitious lot, believe that a Syd sighting is a mark of a surefire theatrical hit.

Who knows? Perhaps the spirit of vaudeville will never truly die.

Spring Garden Road Memorial Public Library

5381 SPRING GARDEN ROAD

N 44°38.63' W 63°34.46'

Those Poor Dead Bones

S INCE 1951, WHEN THE SPRING GARDEN ROAD MEMORIAL PUBLIC Library was first built, visitors and employees have reported sighting an eerie-looking fellow prowling in the stacks. He is dressed in old-fashioned clothing and simply vanishes when approached. Some believe this mysterious figure is one of the eight hundred people who are buried beneath the library grounds.

Digging Deeper

The Spring Garden Road Memorial Public Library, situated on the northwest corner of Spring Garden Road and Grafton Street, has always been a favourite Halifax location for me. It's a lively spot full of pigeons and panhandlers and french fry trucks, not to mention the massive statue of an indomitable Winston Churchill and an entire building full of freely accessible books, music, and movies.

Churchill actually visited our city a couple of times late in the war and, to all reports, loved it. During one speech he led the crowd in an impromptu singalong, bawling out such show-stopping tunes as "It's a Long Way to Tipperary," "O Canada," and "God Save the Queen." He was so impressed with Halifax that as he was boarding the *Queen Mary* to leave he announced, "Now we know that your city is something more than a shed on a wharf."

However, Churchill's Nova Scotia roots ran much deeper. Churchill's great-great-grandmother, Anna Baker, was born in 1761 in Sackville, Nova Scotia. Yes sir and yes ma'am, Winston Churchill had a Bluenose bloodline.

The library was built in 1951 as a monument to commemorate Halifax's World War One and World War Two casualties. And, it was built upon an actual graveyard.

The Poor House

Back in the early 1750s, Halifax was nothing more than a collection of rough log huts lined up along a crosshatch of dirt roads. Those who could afford houses lived in them. Those who couldn't—widows, orphans, broken soldiers too wounded to go to war, the sick, the old, and the mentally infirm—milled about in the daylight foraging for whatever they could find.

By 1758, Halifax had enough of these vagrants. The Governor's Council yielded to the demands of the public and constructed a large, wooden building on the property where the Spring Garden Road Library now stands.

The Poor House looked like a haunted house from an old Hammer horror movie. One expected to see bats and maybe a few gargoyles and a madwoman or two in the attic. In truth, a whipping post and stocks were kept handy on the front lawn. Several times a week, a large ex-slave named Hawkins, proudly wearing the tattered, cast-off green and red uniform of a York Ranger, would tie inmates to the whipping post and attempt to whip the devil out of them.

The Poor House was where you went or you were sent if you couldn't support yourself. Or, as the Joint Committee of Council and Assembly members put it,

> all disorderly and idle persons, and all persons who shall be found begging, or practicing any unlawful game, or pretending to fortune-telling, common drunkards, persons of lewd behaviour, vagabonds, runaways, stubborn servants, apprentices and children, and all persons who notoriously misspend their time to the neglect and prejudice of their own or their family's support...all breakers of the peace, idle or disorderly persons...Sabbath breakers...runaways, or men and women found frequenting any disorderly house or houses of ill fame....

In short, if you didn't fit in with proper society, to the Poor House you would go.

Between the whippings and the time spent leaning in the stocks (or any other punishments the attendants dreamed up), a resident of the Poor House enjoyed a very brief life expectancy. It seemed only sensible to lay out a handy cemetery for the disposal of those residents who died while under its care.

Now mind you, although St. Paul's Cemetery was open directly across the street from the Poor House and was considered "classless," in that you didn't need all that many credentials to be buried there, the folks who lived in the Poor House were considered unwelcome—even in the graveyard.

Instead, they were buried in shallow graves about the grounds of the Poor House. In time folks even began calling it the Poor House Cemetery. Halifax authorities used the grounds to bury the remains of those folks who died in prison or those who were hanged. An entire regiment of Highlanders returning from battle in the American Revolution were stricken with a deadly fever. Most of the men died and while the commanding officers were dutifully buried in St. Paul's Cemetery, the men in the ranks were wrapped in shrouds and buried as quickly as possible in the Poor House Cemetery.

The Rise of the Bridewell

In the year 1814, as the bonfires of Washington's White House were slowly dying and the War of 1812 was winding down, the Poor House was officially converted to a "bridewell," which was another term for a house of correction used mainly for the short-term confinement and punishment of petty offenders and those who were regarded as anti-social misfits—such as vagrants, itinerants, vagabonds, and loose women.

According to Joseph Howe, "the Keeper of the Bridewell was a brute who reigned over the place with harsh cruelty." When Howe visited the bridewell to investigate, he discovered a resident who was wearing a spiked collar around his neck and was chained to the fence as punishment for disobeying the guards. Howe also discovered a woman kept in the pillory all night in the open yard because she would not submit to the brutal embrace of one of the guards. The practice of public floggings, long out of fashion in late eighteenth-century Halifax, was still common at the Poor House, and as a result, the Poor House Cemetery was doing a booming business.

Interment was a rather casual affair. Shallow graves were common and you often might have tripped over an exposed arm or foot—a sort of human speed bump. Plumbing was bad, conditions were worse, and the yard often stank of human refuse.

The Fall of the Bridewell

Eventually the public got tired of the weekly beatings and the all-around ambience of open-air plumbing. People wanted somewhere to walk and some roses to smell. The provincial government agreed to turn the land over to the city of Halifax providing that the property remained a public space in perpetuity.

The building was torn down and the poor folk were transferred to a larger facility on Robie and South. Fill was carted in and the hollow places and offending speed bumps were covered up. Trees and rose-bushes were planted and park benches installed. The location, called Grafton Park at the time, was a small, tree-shaded haven from the hub-bub and commotion of city life. You could picnic here and children could play and lovers could walk through the shadows while below their feet the dead slept on.

Eventually, when the demand for a public library outstripped the need for picnics in the park, the government decided that the provisions attached to the property—that is, the necessity to keep it a public

The Spring Garden Road Memorial Public Library, home to books and ghosts.

place—would not be violated by the construction and opening of a public library.

The public library was designed to be set back far enough to the north of the park so as to allow for the traditional walkway that is still there today.

The Library Ghost

Library employees, especially those who work late in the basement, have sometimes reported seeing shapes and shadows of people moving about in the darkness. Breathing is heard and books are often misplaced. Is it a ghost? Perhaps all of those panhandlers that you see out there leaning against the stone wall of the library are nothing more than spirits of those poor buried souls.

Some believe that the library ghost is nothing more than an urban legend. Others are certain that it is the ghost of a long-forgotten library clerk.

If there is a ghost, I believe it to be the spirit of one of those many poor souls who were buried in unmarked graves beneath these library grounds. With nearly eight hundred souls buried beneath those popular facilities, one wonders how easily they rest while you walk above ground, munching on french fries, over their poor dead bones.

The Old Courthouse

5250 SPRING GARDEN ROAD

N 44°38.63' W 63°34.44'

A Little Gallows Humour

W HEN YOU VISIT THE OLD COURTHOUSE, BE SURE TO CHECK out the interesting carvings above the front doors, but be wary of whoever you might see hanging around, because a court-house employee swears to have seen what may have been the ghost of the last man hanged right here in the backyard of the Old Halifax Courthouse.

Fun for All Ages

Up until the end of the nineteenth century, hangings in Halifax were a popular public occasion. Crowds gathered to watch the sight of a full-grown man or woman dancing their final jig in mid-air. Picnic lunches were often packed. Booths were set up for the peddling of food, and candy for the kids and even toys were sold. It was considered to be a family event.

Even when the hangings took place on board one of the harbour vessels, as often happened if a sailor in the employ of Her Majesty's Navy was to be hanged, the public found a way to enjoy the gruesome entertainment. Spectators rowed out or would pay to be rowed out into the harbour close enough to watch the goings on. A hanging was both an object lesson in grim judgment and a way to pass the time.

Stored somewhere in this old courthouse on Spring Garden Road are the remnants of a town gallows.

However, as twentieth-century sensibilities yielded to the encroachment of civilization and folks became a little more uptight, public hangings were publicly frowned upon and a gallows was set up in the fenced-in backyard of the Old Halifax Courthouse where the authorities could dangle the criminal and unwanted without worries of any public recrimination.

The Last Shoe Drops

On March 7, 1935, the last man to be hanged in the city of Halifax was executed. His name was Daniel P. Sampson. He was a forty-nine-year-old black man who had, by all reports, a diminished mental capacity and some anger management difficulties. Apparently he had been in an argument that day and was carrying his mother's butcher knife when he stumbled upon two boys, aged ten and twelve, picking berries. I'm not sure what sort of berries you would pick in March, but these are the facts as they have been reported.

The boys may have teased him or he may have simply lost his temper. He killed them both and he was convicted and sentenced to hang in the courthouse. He took his punishment calmly, perhaps not even realizing the ramifications of what he was doing or perhaps welcoming the peace that he imagined it would bring him.

He stepped to the gallows, eschewing a blindfold, and waited until the executioner released the trap door. There was a "crack like a pistol shot" and he hung there twisting at the end of Halifax's last gallows rope.

"Well, that is that," one spectator said.

Was it?

They packed up the gallows and put it away; it was never to be used again.

A Promise Kept

Years later, one of the courthouse janitors was ordered to clean up the attic and upper storage rooms. Stored in a dark and eerie room on the top floor of the courthouse were the disassembled pieces of the courthouse gallows, perhaps stored in case of a judicial change of heart or perhaps stored for future posterity.

In any case, the unlucky janitor ran terrified and shaking from the upper room.

"There were eyes in the wood," the janitor swore, "staring at me from out of the darkness."

He would not elaborate upon that statement. He turned in his broom and quit a good government job, swearing to never return to the courthouse again. He was so scared that he resigned his position on that very day.

As far as I know he kept that promise of never returning to the courthouse again.

St. Paul's Cemetery

SPRING GARDEN ROAD & BARRINGTON STREET

N 44°38.62' W 63°34.36'

The Ghost of General Ross

THE GHOST OF MAJOR GENERAL ROBERT ROSS, THE FELLOW WHO helped burn the original White House, is said to prowl the grave-yard grounds brandishing a sword at any who approach him. In addition to the ghost of General Ross, there are an awful lot of stories buried here in Halifax's oldest burial ground.

A Tale Among Tales

Here lies the Body of
MARY WISTON *Daughter of*
ROBERT *&* **SUSANAH WISTON**
who Departed this Life
May the 1st 1778
Aged 3 Years & 5 Weeks
Her time was short, the longer is her Rest
God call'd her hence because he saw it Best
Alas she's gone and like a spotless Dove
To increase the Number of the Blessd Above
Secure of Peace her Soul is gone to Rest
In the eternal Mansions of the Blessd

This is just one of the many stories that you will find recorded upon the crumbling granite tombstones of St. Paul's Old Burying Ground. To find this particular epitaph, enter the front gate of the St. Paul's Old Burying Ground. The very first sight you will see is a huge monument to Halifax's participation in the Crimean War. There is a huge lion atop this monument and an engraving that reads SEBASTOPOL. I will talk a little more about this monument in a few paragraphs, but for now let us use this imposing structure as a landmark to steer by. Just beyond the monument is a dirt path that looks a little like a crossroads—appropriate for a cemetery, I would say. Walk to the end of the crossroads closest to the iron fence, then turn right and walk westward (towards Spring Garden Road) until you are close to the single tree that is opposite the parking sign in the courthouse driveway next door. Little Mary is waiting there for you to read her story and tuck her into bed.

The stories in this graveyard are as endless as the memory of stone. Under a tiny death's head is the cemetery's oldest marked grave, which belongs to two-year-old Malachi Salter Jr. who, in 1752, was tucked into his final resting place.

*These stone markers only adorn about ten percent of the bodies buried
at St. Paul's Cemetery.*

Gravestones back in the eighteenth century were a lot more com-
prehensive in detail than they are today. This was perhaps to make up
for the far too many corpses that were buried in unmarked graves. In
Halifax: Warden of the North, author Thomas H. Raddall describes
how early Haligonians buried their dead in the cemetery: "Here the
dead were thrust away into the frozen earth with little ceremony, and
little or nothing to mark the graves. Like any London cemetery of the
period it was held to be inexhaustible, one generation burying itself
upon another, so that none of the inscribed stones now to be seen there
hark back to the beginning."

According to Raddall, the only form of identification was the set of
carved initials carelessly hacked into a corner of the coffin by a carpen-
ter-caretaker named Vernon.

A Big Neutered Pussycat

Halifax was founded in 1749, and one of its oldest cemeteries, also known as the Old Burying Ground, is St. Paul's on Barrington Street and Spring Garden Road. Some twelve thousand people are buried here, but fewer than 10 percent of their graves are marked. This cemetery was opened in 1749 and was used until 1844 as the burial site for all citizens irrespective of their class and faith—with the exception of the fortunate few who qualified to be interred in the crypts beneath St. Paul's Anglican Church.

It's a gorgeous cemetery with old-fashioned, hand-carved gravestones decorated with such dark subject matter as skulls, crossbones, ravens, bats, the usual angels and flying cherubim, and the like. Upon entering the cemetery, the first thing you will see is an enormous thirty-foot high monument, what Thomas Raddall referred to as "a somewhat ugly brownstone arch," with the stone statue of a lion mounted on top. The monument was raised in 1860 in memory of two Halifax men who perished in the Crimean War—Major A. F. Welsford and Captain W. B. C. A. Parker.

The lion once boasted a proud set of life-size leonine genitalia; however, a few years after the monument was raised, a group of concerned Halifax gentlewomen protested loudly enough until the city council had the offending bit of anatomy chiselled off. Thus, the lion was safely neutered and Halifax could rest easy.

However, not everyone in that graveyard rested easily.

The Rocket's Red Glare

Erected at the public expense to the memory
of Major General Robert Ross
Who, having undertaken and executed an enterprise
against the city of Washington, the capital of
the United States of America, which was crowned
with complete success, was killed shortly
afterwards while directing a successful attack
upon a superior force, near the city of
Baltimore, on the 12ᵗʰ day of September, 1814

This monument in St. Paul's Cemetery honours two men killed in the Crimean War.

To the left of the crossroads, tucked in the center of a huddle of raised tombs beneath a tall, forked poplar, looking like some sort of archaic military emplacement, lies the body of Major General Robert Ross.

Following the defeat of Napoleon, Ross came to North America to take complete charge of all British troops stationed on the eastern coast. He lived in Halifax and led the British forces to victory in the War of 1812, staging a successful attack against the city of Washington, DC.

Prior to the attack, Ross decreed that only public buildings should be subjected to destruction, and so he was responsible for the burning of the White House, and some say, the inspiration behind Francis Scott Key's writing of the American national anthem.

"The rockets' red glare, the bombs bursting in air."

During a subsequent attack on Baltimore, Ross was shot while drawing his sword for a charge. Ross died while being transported back to his ship. To preserve it for burial, his body was stored in a barrel of 129 gallons of dark Jamaican rum. His remains were shipped on the HMS *Royal Oak* and were buried in an above-ground tomb. It's that tall tomb standing regally beneath the forked poplar.

Witnesses have reported seeing the ghost of Major General Robert Ross, on certain dark, moonless nights, striding across the Old Burying Ground and brandishing his sword as if he were ready to make war on a whole horde of invading American tourists.

Have Wheelbarrow, Will Travel

You can also find the grave of Captain James Lawrence of the *Chesapeake* (famous for his cry, "Don't give up the ship") who died before entering Halifax Harbour following his duel with the British frigate *Shannon*. His grave is quite empty, though, since the bones were removed and reburied in New York's famed Trinity Churchyard.

I believe my favourite story dates back to 1787 when Mr. D., the town ferryman, rolled into the Old Burying Ground pushing his wife's dead body in a wheelbarrow not more than five hours after the coroner, one Mr. Gray, had pronounced her dead.

Gray pursued the ferryman and caught up to him in the graveyard to protest his actions.

"It isn't seemly," Gray argued. "The body is not yet cold."

"Nonsense," the old ferryman retorted. "Get on with the digging. She's dead enough, isn't she?"

Waverley Inn

1266 BARRINGTON STREET

N 44°38.45' W 63°34.27'

A Wilde Olde Ghost

THE WAVERLEY INN HAS LONG BEEN THOUGHT TO BE HAUNTED by the rather flamboyant ghost of the infamous Irish playwright, novelist, and poet, Oscar Wilde. He sits there, rather aloofly, in the drawing room just behind the big bay window to the right of the front door, reading a favourite book and perhaps making up for all of that quality reading time he missed while in prison.

A Wilde Tale

Standing on Barrington Street, just between Morris and Harvey streets, is the stylish and atmospheric Waverley Inn—a welcome harbour of gentile, exquisite décor. The Lonely Planet traveller's guidebook describes the Waverley as "a circus for the senses and poetry to the eyes...if film director Tim Burton were to decorate a heritage inn, it would probably end up looking like this one. Think *[The] Adams Family* meets Buckingham Palace. The hallways are lined with dusty-pink satin and gold-threaded wallpaper and old style portraits that keep a steady watch over guests."

However, the eyes of the hanging portraits aren't the only eyes keeping watch in the Waverley Inn. The inn has been doing business here in Halifax since October 1876 and has given shelter to such twentieth-century icons as circus owner P. T. Barnum, financier George Vanderbilt, and of course the famous (or infamous) Irish poet Oscar Wilde.

The friendly front of the Waverley Inn on Barrington Street

Oscar stayed at the Waverley Inn on the first few nights of his 1882 tour of North America. He was described as a flamboyant character, fond of wearing green velvet pantaloons and gold buckle shoes — gaudy apparel, even for that day and age. For a sizable honorarium, Oscar would come to your home and entertain. He was an old-style busker, as well as an author; by all reports he was an accomplished performer.

Oscar Wilde enjoyed his stay in Halifax and swore that he would return; however, fate intervened. In 1895, Oscar's risky and risqué lifestyle was challenged publicly. He stood trial back in England and on May 25, 1895, was convicted of gross indecency and sentenced to two years of hard labour. Prison life was rough on Oscar and after he was released he spent his last few years in poverty and obscurity.

Even in death he went out with a touch of panache. He was quoted as saying on his deathbed, "My wallpaper and I are fighting a duel to the death. One or other of us has to go."

Apparently the wallpaper won out.

Wilde was buried in the notorious Père-Lachaise Cemetery, along with the likes of Chopin, Proust, and Jim Morrison, the lead singer of The Doors. Wilde's body was reportedly immersed in quicklime and buried in a quiet, unmarked grave before public burial, in order to deter possible graveyard violation. However, after a nine-year immersion in the quicklime, Oscar's body refused to rot. Perhaps he was one of those rare, saintly, and incorruptible-type people. Perhaps he was merely too stubborn to rot. Whatever the case, his corpse was eventually buried in his grand, self-designed, and highly ostentatious tomb at Père-Lachaise.

Oscar's Return to Halifax

The revenant spirit of Oscar Wilde has been seen time and time again at the Waverley Inn. Witnesses describe him as being garishly dressed. He is often seen standing and reading a book. He was a tall man and probably found it uncomfortable to hunker down for too long upon a normal-sized chair. The owners of the Waverley Inn have further preserved the author's memory by naming one of the rooms after him—presumably the room in which he stayed. Visitors swear that they have seen his ghost standing at the doorway to the Oscar Wilde room, number 122.

Do you dare spend a night at the Waverley? If you do spend the night and are visited by the ghost of Oscar Wilde, do ask him to quote a little of his poetry.

Holy Cross Cemetery

SOUTH STREET & SOUTH PARK STREET

N 44°38.32' W 63°34.61'

The *Saladin* Massacre

IN THE YEAR 1844, A BAND OF A HALF-DOZEN RUTHLESS MUTINEERS were arrested and hanged in Halifax. Their crime was the cold-blooded massacre of the captain and half of the crew of the *Saladin* for the sake of a cargo of silver and gold. They were convicted in what was Nova Scotia's last major piracy trial. The six men were hanged at the far end of the South Commons, or what we now call Victoria Park. Their ghosts are said to walk the grounds of the nearby Holy Cross Cemetery in which some of them were buried. The story here centres on a grave that has long been unmarked, so I cannot direct you to any particular part of the graveyard. However, the tale is a dark and fascinating chapter in Halifax history and well worth hearing.

Enter the Villain

Scoundrel, rogue, and most determined villain, Captain George Fielding set sail in October 1842 from Liverpool, England, as the captain of the barque *Vitula*.

Fielding's latest enterprise, an attempt to smuggle a load of seabird guano—a prime ingredient in fertilizer and more importantly, gunpowder—without paying the necessary legal fees, seemed an easy way to make a cheap buck. Docking in Peru, however, Fielding was met by a longboat full of Peruvian soldiers.

"Surrender your vessel," the Peruvian captain commanded.

Fielding handed out arms to his crew; however, his crew hid in the hold, intent on saving their own skins. Unaided, Fielding desperately attempted to cut his anchor rope with a carving knife, but a Peruvian soldier put a musket ball in Fielding's shoulder, thus ending his attempt at escape.

The *Vitula* was seized and Fielding and his crew were thrown into the jail at Callo, Peru. Fielding's incarceration didn't last long. With the help of his teenage son, Fielding escaped the jailhouse, hiding out on the local waterfront until hope arrived in the shape of another British barque.

The *Saladin*

That barque was the *Saladin*, a 550-ton British barque distinguished by its gaudily carved figurehead—a bronze bust of the old Kurdish sultan Saladin—complete with turban, earrings, and a marvellous bushy moustache. The *Saladin* sailed into Callo Bay for a routine resupply; it was heavily laden with a cargo of thirteen 150-pound bars of silver, twenty tons of copper, some spices, the ever-popular bird guano, and an iron chest of gold pieces.

Fielding talked his way on board the *Saladin*, claiming to have been the victim of corrupt port authorities. Captain Alexander Mackenzie, master of the *Saladin*, gave Fielding and his son sanctuary at a price.

"You can work your passage off," Mackenzie offered.

The offer wasn't enough for Fielding. He chafed at taking orders from Mackenzie, who was a hard-headed, tough-minded seadog who enforced his commands with bellows, curses, or solid, well-aimed kicks. Fielding smiled and accepted Mackenzie's offer, silently vowing to turn the tables as soon as he could.

There could only be one captain on board the *Saladin* and as far as Captain George Fielding was concerned, he would be that captain.

A Peg Leg, a Perfect Pirate, and a Pup

Once the vessel had rounded Cape Horn and reached the mid-Atlantic, Fielding made his move. He convinced four crewmen to mutiny: Jack Hazelton, Bill Trevaskis, Charles Gustavus Anderson, and George Jones.

George Jones was the first recruit. He was a one-legged Irishman who had been picked on by Mackenzie from the start. The second was an American named John Hazelton—a twenty-eight-year-old sailor described by witnesses at the trial as a man who bore the physical look of "a perfect pirate." Little is known of the third accomplice, Trevaskis, who was travelling under the name of Johnson for his own reasons.

Charles Gustav Anderson was the youngest mutineer. He was a Swede who spoke in broken English, was the son of a prosperous master shipbuilder, and was, by all accounts, quite well educated. At nineteen, he was the youngest of the conspirators, not counting Fielding's teen-age son. Anderson was nothing more than a puppy, really, and I wonder if he was not simply misled by the pressures of his older shipmates.

Still, talking the four men into a mutiny wasn't hard. Captain Mackenzie wasn't liked much and the silver, gold, and copper cargo inflamed their greed.

Events came to a head in April on Friday the 13th—a day of bad luck for the *Saladin*. Fielding and his gang decided mutiny and murder were the only proper course.

On the following night they decided to act.

The Mutiny

The attack occurred during the middle watch, which takes place between midnight and four in the morning. The mutineers reasoned most sailors would be asleep and the crew on duty would be groggy and easy to fool. Fielding, Trevaskis, Jones, and Anderson picked up a claw hammer, a maul, an adze, and a broadaxe from the ship's carpenter's tool chest.

They were ready for battle.

The first mate, Thomas Byerby, had been ill that night and had laid down upon the ship's hen coop and had fallen asleep. While he slumbered, Fielding crept up and smashed his skull in with the blunt end of the broad axe. Three of the mutineers heaved the body of the mate overboard.

"That is one gone," Fielding said.

They stole below deck to the captain's cabin but were turned back by the growling of the ship's dog that always slept at the captain's door.

"What shall we do?" Jones wondered aloud.

"I have a plan," Fielding assured him.

They called the second mate up from his sleep. Anderson struck from behind with the claw hammer just hard enough to stun. The mutineers heaved the incapacitated second mate over the rail.

The splash in the cold ocean revived the semi-conscious second mate as Fielding had planned. The drowning man cried out for help. The mutineers called for Captain Mackenzie. "Man overboard," the cry rang out.

Captain Mackenzie lumbered up from his cabin, shouting a bleary order to turn the ship about, when Fielding struck him in the chest with the broadaxe.

Mackenzie shrugged off the blow and waded into the mutineers, attempting to subdue them single-handedly. His valiant struggle was in vain. Anderson and Jones immobilized the captain as Fielding rained axe blows down upon the helpless skipper.

It was a massacre.

"Give it to him," Fielding's young son George cheered his father on. "Give it to the old bastard."

They finished the captain off and threw him overboard to join his first and second mates at the bottom of the Atlantic. The grey sharks of the Atlantic fed well that night.

"The vessel is now ours," Fielding said. "I am captain."

There were still five crewmen asleep below deck unaware of the butchery going on above them. Hazelton took the wheel. Jones lay down in the ship's boat and Anderson leaned against the mainmast pretending to doze. Trevaskis went forward to call up the next crew member with Fielding and son close behind. The boy carried a carving knife concealed behind his back.

The fourth victim proved as easy to kill as the other three. He was standing on the stern, relieving himself in the ocean below, when Anderson struck him down with a heavy blow from the adze.

"Shall we call for the others?" Jones asked.

"Let the ship do our work for us," Fielding said. "Haul down the flying jib."

The sound of the jib being lowered brought two more crewmen up from their sleep. Before they could do anything, Fielding and his gang finished them off and threw them over the side with the others. The two men that were left were the cook, William Carr, and his young steward, John Galloway.

"We need a cook and a cook needs a steward," Fielding said. "If you two take orders from us we will let you live and give you a half share of the cargo."

Carr and Galloway surrendered without a fight. Privately, Fielding told the others he would personally see that the cook and steward were poisoned before they got to land.

The Double-Cross

Afterwards the mutineers celebrated by ransacking the ship, getting drunk, and throwing the carpenter's tools and the cutlasses and muskets from the captain's cabin overboard. However, Fielding kept a musket and a cutlass for himself.

"To shoot birds," he told the others. "In case our provisions grow low."

One night later, Fielding asked Galloway to join him and his son in the overthrow of the rest of the mutineers.

"Why split all of that plunder amongst the others?" he asked, doubtlessly hoping that the young steward would be easily misled.

However, before Fielding could begin his planned massacre, Hazelton and Trevaskis found two more pistols, a carving knife, and a bottle of poison hidden in Fielding's locker.

The mutineers seized Fielding and bound his hands and feet. They kept him gagged for a while, debating what to do. Finally, they threw Fielding overboard. Then they ordered the cook and the steward to murder Fielding's son. It took some doing, but finally Carr and Galloway gave in and threw the young man overboard.

"Now you're one of us," Jones said.

Without captain or compass, the mutineers made their way northward.

"We'll scuttle the ship off Cape Breton," Jones decided, "and travel by longboat up the Gulf of St. Lawrence."

They did their best to camouflage the ship—nailing a board over the name *Saladin* and whitewashing the distinctive bronze figurehead. They also threw the copper and the guano overboard, reasoning that the ship would travel faster without the added weight. Besides, there was no room in the longboat for all of that copper. The silver and the gold would have to do.

Privately, some men wondered what else could be thrown overboard.

What else, or who else?

Coming to Justice

On the Wednesday morning of May 22, 1844, the *Saladin* ran aground on Harbour Island about a hundred miles east of the mouth of Halifax Harbour. The authorities saw through the fogbank of lies and misinformation that the mutineers attempted to hide behind. The lot of them were brought to Halifax to stand trial and were confined at the Melville Island prison.

Galloway and Carr asked for a lawyer's representation and made a complete confession. The rest of the mutineers crumbled quickly. They were charged with murder and sentenced to be hanged after a fifteen-minute deliberation from the appointed jury.

Galloway and Carr were declared innocent. The judge decided they had been forced into their actions. Taking the life of Fielding's son had been an act of self-defence.

The gallows were erected at the far end of the South Common—what is now known as Victoria Park—across the street from the Holy Cross Cemetery. A large crowd of onlookers gathered. The authorities wisely ordered a company of the Fifty-second Regiment to form a protective circle about the gallows to keep the hanging safely under control. The sight of that many armed soldiers with fixed bayonets was enough to contain the crowd.

At ten o'clock in the morning of July 30, 1844, the mutineers travelled down Tower Road in a prison wagon. Everything had been carefully prepared. Their coffins, carefully measured and constructed, were placed out below the gallows, waiting for them to drop on in. The cutthroats were terrified. Only the young Swede, Charles Gustav Anderson, seemed indifferent to the situation.

"Gustav stood perfectly erect and gazed around on the vast assemblage," one witness reported.

The hangman paused to give them time to say their last farewells. They shook hands and Jones kissed each of his buddies on the cheek and told the crowd that he was sorry for what he'd done.

"I hope to find pardon from God," he said.

And then the white cotton hoods were pulled over their heads, the clergyman walked from the gallows, and the trap door opened. The four men who killed together died together. Trevaskis and Anderson kicked for a moment. The other two broke clean and went quietly to their death. Their bodies were left to hang there in the morning sunshine for an hour before their remains were hauled away for burial.

The Ghost of Holy Cross Cemetery

Anderson was buried in the potter's field where the Spring Garden Road Memorial Public Library now stands. A Halifax medical student unearthed Anderson's shallow grave that night and carted his cadaver

The rolling fog creates a spooky effect at Holy Cross Cemetery on South Street.

to a dissection room for closer study. The skull was apparently preserved and kept on display in the provincial museum for a while.

Trevaskis was buried alongside Anderson. Although Anderson came from a wealthy Swedish family, they left him to his fate. As Roman Catholics, Hazelton and Jones were buried in an unmarked section of the Holy Cross Cemetery set aside for execution victims or duellists.

The ghosts of the mutineers, perhaps joined by Fielding and his son, have been seen walking amongst the gravestones. They walked heavily and slowly, their souls weighted with fathomless guilt, carrying a hammer, an adze, a maul, and a carpenter's broadaxe—ready for another grim massacre.

Victoria General Hospital

1278 TOWER ROAD

N 44°38.28' W 63°34.79'

The Old Grey Nun

THE VICTORIA GENERAL HOSPITAL IS SAID TO BE HAUNTED BY THE spirit of an old nun dressed in a long, grey habit. No one seems to know her name or where she originally came from, and folks can't even say which floor or wing of the hospital you will find her on. One thing is for certain; if you are suffering she will be there. The grey nun is said to visit the bedside of certain dying patients to see them safely across to the other side.

What's in the History Books?

The Victoria General Hospital began operations in 1844; however, it wasn't until 1859 that the first actual building was raised. Back then it was known simply as the City Hospital. It was closed for a time when the city council lacked the money to keep it running.

The Victoria General Hospital on Tower Road dates back to 1867.

The building remained empty while the politicians played Ping-Pong with their budget plans. However, in 1867 the numbers came together nicely and the City Hospital re-opened once and for all with the combined support of the City of Halifax and the Province of Nova Scotia.

It took them that long to get it right.

The hospital has been open for business ever since, and some say that it's haunted.

Bonnie's Story

This story was told to me by a tour guide who had heard it from a friend, so it's kind of a hand-me-down. I have seen it mentioned in a few ghost story collections but have never seen it told quite this way.

It began one lonely, moonlit Halifax night. A nurse named Bonnie was making her rounds at the Victoria General Hospital. She carried a flashlight from room to room, checking on the patients, checking their pulses, and making sure they were still breathing. She was a new recruit and was trying hard to do her job as well as she could.

There was an old gentleman patient by the name of Edgar whom she had really grown to care about. Truth to tell, he reminded her of her own dead father. Bonnie was worried about Edgar. She knew that it was only a matter of time, and being a nurse she also knew that it was foolish to allow herself to become emotionally involved in the patient's welfare, but she couldn't help herself. He was a sweet old man and Bonnie felt bad that his family lived too far away to visit him all that often.

When she came to Edgar's room that night she was surprised to see that he wasn't alone.

"I saw an old nun standing over Edgar's bedside, looking down on him," Bonnie described the scene to the head nurse the next morning. "The nun placed her hand upon Edgar's brow. Her lips were moving softly as if she were praying to herself."

Bonnie didn't disturb the two. She told herself that the nun must have come on her own or perhaps she'd been summoned to Edgar's bedside by concerned family members. Still, there was something strange about that lonely midnight vigil.

"There was a soft grey light filling the room," Bonnie said. "It was like the soft grey of early morning when the fog rises up from the sea. The light was bright enough for me not to need my flashlight to see by. As I watched, I felt a feeling rising up inside me like I was saying goodbye to an old friend without ever saying a word."

She paused to take a breath.

"I closed my eyes as if someone had turned on a light too suddenly," Bonnie went on. "When I opened them again the nun was gone. I could smell a slight trace of incense in the air, like the kind they burn in church. When I stepped into the room I saw that Edgar was gone as well. He had died, and he was smiling a soft kind of smile as if he'd just shared a joke and a chat with a very old friend."

The head nurse smiled.

"We've been seeing her around here for an awful lot of years," the head nurse said. "Some people think she was a nun who worked here in World War One and was killed in the Halifax Explosion."

And then the head nurse grew strangely quiet.

"Have you ever seen her?" Bonnie finally asked.

"No," the head nurse replied. "I haven't. I've worked with a few nurses who say they have seen her, but I haven't seen her myself."

Bonnie thought on that.

Then it was her turn to smile.

"I believe I'll see her again," Bonnie said. "I'm sure I'll see her just one more time before it's time for me to go home."

Bonnie has since passed on, the tour guide told me. I wonder sometimes if just before she died she looked up and saw a pale, soft, twilight grey nun looking down on her and praying softly to herself.

Point Pleasant Park

Remembering the Battle

WHEN YOU FIRST LOOK, THERE ISN'T ALL THAT MUCH TO SEE — just a grey granite wedge, about eight feet tall, in Point Pleasant Park on the ocean side of Sailor's Memorial Way. It's a monument to commemorate the battle of the *Shannon* and the *Chesapeake*.

If you are here on a proper night you might see a more fitting monument to the battle out on the waves of Halifax Harbour. Many witnesses have watched and seen a fully rigged, spectral tall ship sailing into Halifax Harbour and passing slowly through the channel between Point Pleasant Park and McNabs Island. Some believe it to be a ghostly revisitation of the crew and captain of the American frigate *Chesapeake* seeking one more shot at their archrival, the HMS *Shannon*.

An Honourable Confrontation

Let's take you back to the morning of June 1, 1813. The War of 1812 was one year old and the British had still not managed to gain a single victory in ship-to-ship action. The navy was beginning to get worried. Perhaps Britannia did not rule the waves quite as completely as they had once believed.

It was a bright and sunny Tuesday morning as Captain Philip Broke, the commanding officer of the fifty-two-cannon British frigate *Shannon*, waited patiently at the mouth of Boston Harbour for the American frigate the *Chesapeake* to set sail and meet him in battle on the open sea.

"I don't quite understand why you bothered sending the enemy a warning message," First Lieutenant T. L. Watts said to Captain Broke.

Captain Broke smiled with the barest of indulgence. As captain of the *Shannon*, Broke was not inclined nor expected to explain his orders. However, he was going into what promised to be one hell of a battle. First Lieutenant Watts was a good man with a cool head and Broke wanted him on his side.

"In the last short while the damned Americans have taken the HMS *Guerriere, Macedonian, Java*, and *Peacock*." Broke explained. "And we haven't managed to take a single one of their warships."

"Aye, sir." Watts replied.

"Those were British ships, sir. They were taken as easily as I might pluck my hat from atop my head," Broke went on, using the excuse of a metaphor to raise his hat and wipe the summer sweat from his brow. "We're losing this naval war here in Canada. We need to show the world what the British navy is capable of."

"I understand, sir."

"Do you?" Broke asked. "We need a victory—an undeniable victory—and so I have tracked the American *Chesapeake* to this harbour and I plan to engage her in battle. I plan to beat her, sir, and I need this to be a fair and honourable and indisputable victory—frigate against frigate, cannon against cannon."

"So you sent him a message, sir."

Broke smiled grimly.

"I sent him no message," Broke shook his head. "I sent him a challenge that no honourable captain could refuse."

"Quite sporting of you, sir," Watts agreed grudgingly.

"This isn't sport, First Lieutenant," Broke corrected. "This is war. I want that ship and I want the damned newspapers to know about it."

Training and Drills

Broke was confident and he had every right to be. He knew full well that Captain Lawrence of the *Chesapeake* was equally as aggressive and honour-bound as Broke himself.

Besides that, the *Shannon*'s crew was one of the hardest and best-drilled crews in either the British or the American navy. Broke had relentlessly trained his men daily over the last several years, performing live gunnery drills. Broke's insistence on live gunnery drills may have been the deciding factor. At this time, gunnery drills in both navies were frequently performed without shot or powder to save on the cost. Broke was obsessed with the science of artillery. He trained his men relentlessly, demanding the use of powder and shot in every training exercise.

"Damn the powder shortage," he swore. "My gunners need to be used to the kick and the roar and the smoke of actual battle."

By 1813, Broke's men may have actually been the best-trained tars in either navy. It is perhaps arguable whether or not Broke was aware of this fact when he set loose a surrendered American captain by the name of Slocum in a ship's boat into Boston Harbour to issue the *Shannon*'s challenge to the *Chesapeake*.

The Challenge

"As the *Chesapeake*," Broke wrote in his challenge to Lawrence, the *Chesapeake*'s captain, "appears now ready for sea, I request that you will do me the favour to meet the *Shannon* with her, ship-to-ship."

Broke proceeded to explain the exact armament of the *Shannon*, the number of crew on board, the interesting circumstance that Broke was short of provisions and water, and the fact that he had sent away his consort ship, the HMS *Tenados*, with orders to search for the *Chesapeake* wherever it was not so that the two could fight one-on-one.

"If you will favour me," Broke went on to say, "with any plan of signals or telegraph, I will warn you should any of my friends be too nigh, while you are in sight, until I can detach them out of the way. Or," he suggested coaxingly, "I would sail under a flag of truce to anyplace you think safest from our cruisers, hauling it down when fair, to begin hostilities…. Choose your terms," he concluded, "but let us meet."

Having sent out this amazing letter, this middle-aged, unromantic, but hard-fighting captain climbed at daybreak to his own maintop crow's nest and stood there as eagerly as a boy waiting for a birthday party. He watched the challenged ship sitting in Boston Harbour to see if its foretopsail would be unloosed and it would come out for a fight.

The Best-Laid Plans

Unfortunately, Captain Lawrence and the *Chesapeake* never received the challenge. It was lost in the red tape that Slocum, the released American, encountered upon entering Boston Harbour.

The *Shannon* continued to wait.

It was a calm morning and a fair sea. The sun was shining and the crew of the *Shannon* could see the *Chesapeake* moored in Boston Harbour. The *Shannon* rested in the deeper waters within telescope range of the harbour. At this time there weren't many warships commissioned in the United States Navy. Broke knew he needn't worry about being outnumbered. It was only a matter of waiting.

There were many merchant ships in Boston Harbour and Broke could have had his pick of any of them, but he wasn't here for plunder. He was here for glory and battle. He was here for the *Chesapeake*.

However, the *Chesapeake* didn't seem to be interested in battle this morning. It sat there with its sails furled and wasn't going anywhere. Broke wasn't worried. He was a patient man and he knew that sooner or later the *Chesapeake* must sail.

At ten o'clock, Broke called general quarters and set the men to target practice, as was his custom. One wonders what the men of the *Chesapeake* thought, sitting there in that harbour looking out to sea, as their enemy practised marksmanship.

An hour and a half later, Broke climbed slowly down from his post on the maintop mast. He was feeling a little dejected at the time. He had been certain that the *Chesapeake* would meet him today.

"Perhaps she didn't receive your challenge," Watts said.

Broke shook his head, refusing to admit the fallibility of his scheme.

"They must have it by now," he said. "Perhaps they are afraid."

"We could sail in and get them," Watts suggested.

"And lose our open sea? We'd be cut to pieces by the harbour guns and boarded and towed by their smaller boats," he shook his head grimly. "No sir, the next move is certainly that of the *Chesapeake*."

At that moment, as if in answer, the *Chesapeake's* sails slowly unfurled.

"She is coming out," Watts said.

Broke only smiled softly.

"Good," he said. "Let him come."

An Unassuming Ship

Knowing that it would take at least two hours for the *Chesapeake* to draw close enough for battle, Broke retired to his cabin. For the next hour the men stood by their cannons watching anxiously as the American ship approached. What Broke was thinking during that hour he sat behind the closed door of his cabin is anybody's guess. Perhaps he was merely napping.

In any case, an hour later, Broke stepped back out of his cabin and spoke to the crew.

"Shannons!" he called out. "You know that the Americans have lately triumphed over British frigates. But they have gone further than that. They have published in their newspapers that the English have forgotten how to fight."

He let that sink in.

"You will let them know today that there are Englishmen on the *Shannon* who still know how to fight."

The men roared their approval fiercely.

Broke waited for the uproar to subside.

"Do not try to demast her. Fire into her quarters, main deck into main deck, quarterdeck into quarterdeck," he instructed. "Kill the men and the ship is yours!"

That brought on another bloodthirsty commotion. Broke held up his hands for silence.

"We will fight in dignified silence," he told them. "Don't cheer. Don't curse. Go quietly to your quarters and do your duty. Remember, you have the blood of hundreds of your countrymen to avenge."

One of the crewmen asked if they might fly three battle flags, as the *Chesapeake* was that day, instead of the single flag that the *Shannon* usually flew.

"No," Broke replied. "We have always been an unassuming ship."

Well, it wasn't exactly "Remember the Alamo!" but it certainly did the job.

The *Chesapeake* continued its slow approach as the men of the *Shannon* made themselves ready for war.

The Battle

By 3:40 PM, the first shot of the battle was fired by the *Shannon*. The *Chesapeake* had sailed alongside the *Shannon* without firing a shot. Captain Lawrence was as eager as Broke to keep this battle fair and honourable.

Broke, assuming that Lawrence had already received his personally delivered challenge, was under no compunction to hold his fire. He had been waiting for this chance all morning long and he wasn't about to miss it.

"Fire at will into her quarters," Broke ordered.

The first gun to fire belonged to the *Shannon*. It was its Number Fourteen gun, positioned on its main deck and commanded by one Billy Mindham, Broke's coxswain.

The shot was a good one, blasting away an entire gun crew aboard the *Chesapeake*. Then, like a row of dominoes tipping over one by one, the guns of the *Shannon* erupted in a burst of smoke, shot, and flame.

A hurricane of splinters, ball, rope, and wreckage blasted across the deck of the *Chesapeake* turning the ordered ship into a charnel house. Of the 150 men at battle stations upon the *Chesapeake*, over a hundred were killed or wounded, including Captain Lawrence who was shot through the abdomen by the lucky musket shot of a young English marine by the name of Lieutenant Low.

Seeing his captain fall, Lieutenant William Cox sprang into action. He scooped up Captain Lawrence in his arms and carried him off the deck down to the ship's surgeon. This heroic action cost him dearly. A few months later, Cox would be court-martialled by a United States board of inquiry eager for some sort of a scapegoat. Cox was charged and dismissed from service for leaving his post to take his captain below deck.

"Tell the men to fire faster," Lawrence ordered from the surgeon's table. "Don't give up the ship."

The *Chesapeake* returned fire with equal determination. However, the training of Broke's crew and their readiness for battle proved irresistible. The two ships closed to pistol-shot range and the *Shannon* lowered a gangplank.

"Follow me who can," Captain Broke coolly called out, drawing his cutlass as he stepped between the two ships as calmly as if he were stepping out for a Sunday stroll. He was followed

The monument on Sailor's Way commemorates the battle of the Shannon *and the* Chesapeake.

by a boarding party of thirty-two British seamen and eighteen marines. They were armed with pistols, hatchets, cutlasses, and daggers. Anything that could kill was called into play as they stepped out to confront the much larger American crew. Even after the deadly barrage, it was estimated that there were still a good 270 unwounded American fighting men on board the *Chesapeake*.

Other sailors stepped lively, lashing the ships together as the determined British sailors hacked their way through the American forces. Lieutenant Watts ran onto the ship and tore one of the American flags down. He tried to string up a Union Jack in its place.

In the confusion of battle, one of the gunners on board the *Shannon* saw Watts with the American flag tucked under his arm and mistook him for the enemy. The gunner opened fire and blew the top of the lieutenant's skull off with a blast of grapeshot that also took the lives of four other British sailors.

Meanwhile, Captain Broke was facing his own difficulties. A group of surrendering Americans spotted the British captain standing alone on the *Chesapeake's* forecastle. Three of the Americans snatched up the weapons they had just dropped in surrender and attacked Broke.

Broke calmly parried one sailor's attack and then slashed the sailor's left cheek open with a slice of his cutlass. A second sailor tried to shoot Broke, but his musket misfired. Instead, he stepped up and hammered the British captain's skull with the butt end of his musket. At the same time, a pistol shot took Broke in the shoulder. Broke dropped to his knees. Another American slashed wildly at Broke, knocking the captain's hat askew and carving a slice from his scalp; one onlooker described it as laying Broke's head open down to the brain.

Broke ignored the gory wound. He fought his way clear, parrying and slashing in a mad blur of motion and slaying all of his attackers as the bulk of the British boarding party reached his side. As his own men came to his rescue, Broke fainted from loss of blood and was rowed back to the *Shannon*. He was unconscious at the moment of victory.

The Aftermath

Tuesday, June 1, 1813
Off Boston Harbour, Northwest of Lawrence
PM: *Took Chesapeake*

Those three lines transcribed from Captain Broke's personal journal do little to sum up the full extent of this battle. The opening broadside attack lasted six short minutes. In those half-dozen minutes, the *Shannon* was blasted by an estimated 158 cannonballs while the *Chesapeake* was riddled with no less than 362 shots.

The boarding of the *Chesapeake* took seven more minutes. In those thirteen minutes, a total of 252 men, British and American, were killed or wounded, making this one of the bloodiest frigate-to-frigate battles in the war. Both captains were badly wounded. Lasting four whole days before passing away just short of the harbour's mouth, Lawrence would not live to see the shores of Halifax.

With himself badly wounded and First Lieutenant Watts dead, Captain Broke had to give command of the *Shannon* over to Lieutenant Provo William Wallis. Wallis was only twenty-two years old, was born and raised in Halifax, and was thrilled and honoured to have been given such a responsibility. Wallis went on in the navy to become an admiral before passing away at the ripe old age of one hundred.

Interrupted Church Service

It was a quiet Sunday morning when Lieutenant Provo William Wallis sailed the *Shannon* into Halifax Harbour. Folks were at worship in St. Paul's Anglican Church. The word spread quickly and soon the entire congregation and the clergy as well were running down the street to the harbour's edge to watch as the *Shannon* guided the beaten *Chesapeake* into home waters.

Just the sight of the vessels looked like something from out of an old horror comic book. As a youth of seventeen, Thomas Haliburton, who would eventually grow up to write the adventures of *Sam Slick*,

Yankee Clockmaker, boarded the vessels with an assortment of onlookers and graphically described what he saw there: "The deck had not been cleaned and the coils and folds of rope were steeped in gore as if in a slaughterhouse. She (the *Chesapeake*) was a fir-built ship and her splinters had wounded nearly as many as the *Shannon*'s shot. Pieces of skin and hair were adhering to the sides of the ship; and in one place I noticed portions of fingers protruding, as if thrust through the outer walls of the frigate; while several sailors…were lying asleep on the bloody floor."

The Ghost of the Harbour

Since then, the ghost of the *Chesapeake*, its sails unfurled and its cannons ready, has been seen sailing beneath the heavenly lantern of a fat full moon on hot June nights, moving straight into the mouth of Halifax Harbour. Perhaps it is looking for one more shot at the *Shannon*.

Shirreff Hall

6385 SOUTH STREET

N 44°38.08' W 63°35.67'

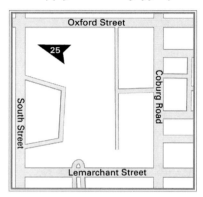

Poor, Poor Penelope

A COLD BLAST OF AIR WELCOMES DALHOUSIE STUDENTS AND visitors alike to the fourth floor of the Shirreff Hall residence. The hall is reputedly haunted by the ghost of a young servant girl who hanged herself up there after being badly treated by one of the professors.

A Generous Gift

Shortly after World War One, Jennie Shirreff Eddy, a wealthy widow and former nurse, stepped forward in an effort to redress the problem of the lack of residence space for Dalhousie's female students. She pledged $300,000 to the building of a new female residence in honour of her parents.

In 1921, the new residence was built as close to Oxford Street as possible in order to preserve the white pine, oak, and maple trees that were common in the area. The residence has been remodelled and expanded over the years and it continues to give good service and safe, comfortable shelter to many Dalhousie students.

Over the years, the story of Penelope, the ghost of Shirreff Hall, has been told and retold.

Is it hearsay or history?

Shirreff Hall as seen from South Street

A Broken Heart

Back in the late 1920s, a young woman named Penelope worked as a maid up on the third and fourth floors of Dalhousie's Shirreff Hall. She was a drab, lonely girl who spoke little and had long, straight, black hair that was already smoked with a hide-and-go-seek of grey even though she was only in her twenties.

"Almost like a ghost, she was," one of the deans was heard to say. "You hardly ever heard her say 'boo.'"

There are a lot of lonely people like that in the world and given time, even the loneliest seem to manage to find someone. Too bad Penelope happened to find the likes of Duncan.

Duncan was a teacher working at the college for a single year. He was a little older and was wise enough to know a good thing when he saw it. He wooed Penelope and sweet-talked her, but when he said they'd be together forever he had his fingers crossed behind his back. Penelope gave her love to the man and when his teaching term was over, he packed his bags and boarded a train without so much as a bye or a leave.

Penelope's tears fell like bitter April rain. She had no one to turn to. To make matters worse, she was pregnant.

She would lose her position and her reputation if word got out.

They found her diary burned in a small pile of ashes beneath the hanging body of poor, poor Penelope—high in an attic where the tattered end of the rope she tied around a beam still hangs.

The students still talk about her and dismiss her tale as just a freshman-year ghost story, but more than a few students have been greeted with a blast of unexpected cool air as they enter the fourth floor. Penelope is still seen sometimes as a shadow walking down the hallway, and footsteps are often heard in the night. Others speak of feeling a sensation of being watched or awakening to see the shape of a young girl standing at the foot of their beds.

University of King's College

6350 COBURG ROAD

N 44°38.27' W 63°35.70'

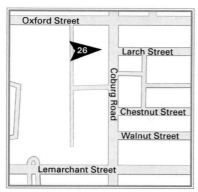

The Phantom of the Pit

T HE PIT IS THE NICKNAME FOR THE SMALL UNDERGROUND theatre that lies underneath the King's College Chapel. For many years the students have told and retold the story of how the Pit is haunted by the ghost of a janitor who is known only by the bright yellow work jacket that he always seems to wear.

In addition to the janitor, the spirit of a strange young girl apparently haunts the college as well. This apparition has been witnessed and reported in the college newspaper as recently as January 2008.

A Brief History

I attended the University of King's College in my early years in Halifax, so I'm glad to have found a ghost story, no matter how brief, from there.

The college was originally founded in Windsor, Nova Scotia, in 1789. In 1802, they received a charter from King George III. However, in the year 1920 a fierce fire burnt the college to the ground.

Phoenix-like, the college rose from the ashes and was rebuilt in Halifax thanks to a grant from the Carnegie Foundation of New York and an agreement they worked out with neighbouring Dalhousie University. The University of King's College is the oldest English-speaking commonwealth university outside the United Kingdom.

And the University of King's College is haunted.

Down in the Pit

The Pit is the nickname that is given by University of King's College students to the area hidden beneath the college chapel. I used to play guitar down there at a talent night that we called the King's College Coffeehouse. It was a lot of years ago and believe you me, my guitar playing was scary enough to chase out any ghosts. However, there is one ghost that will not be scared away even by my guitar playing.

Perhaps he's tone deaf.

The Pit is said to be haunted by the ghost of an old man—a janitor some folk say. He always wears a dirty, yellow work jacket. He has been seen down there moving around chairs and sweeping. However, any time he is seen he quickly disappears.

Like most ghosts he's shy, I guess.

A local team of paranormal researchers spent one entire October night in 2007 down in the depths of the Pit. However, their investigations were inconclusive.

"Except for almost having my video camera stolen and not being able to turn off the lights," investigator Rob Fader reports, "nothing unexplained happened to us during the night. No strange data was captured on our analog and digital cameras, video cameras, or audio recorders.

There were no fluctuations in EMF readings or temperature."

Since that night, at least one more recorded ghost sighting occurred in the University of King's College.

A Later Report

In February 2008, the *Dalhousie Gazette* reported a sighting of a ghost at the University of King's College. Second-year journalism and international development student, Denise Gow, swears that a ghost appeared in her residence room on the third floor of Cochran Bay on the evening of Wednesday, January 16, 2008.

Denise, described by her friends as a level-headed and confident student, claimed that she had been feeling strangely out of sorts all that day.

The University of King's College Arts and Adminstration Building. Cochran Bay Residence is on the right.

"Throughout the day I was really uneasy being in my room," she said. "I kept hearing someone's voice."

Determined to get to the bottom of whatever was happening, Denise systematically investigated the eerie phenomenon. She opened her door and looked up and down the staircase. She looked out of the window to see if it was someone on the floor below her. When the voice persisted, she unplugged her television set, radio, and computer.

"They were all off," she said, "and I was still hearing the voice."

When she returned from her class, things got even stranger.

"I kept hearing the voice a couple of times every ten minutes or so," she said. "I was getting really upset and I thought, 'Okay, I'm going to bed.'"

She turned off the lights and lay down around eleven o'clock, but she still couldn't fall asleep.

"I could have sworn I kept seeing something," she said.

However, it was more than just seeing something. She sensed it in the same way a person might sense someone standing and watching just beyond their field of vision.

"Did you ever have that feeling where your eyes are closed and you have a friend in the room and you know they're by your dresser but you can kind of feel them as they go around the room?" she explained. "It was kind of like that."

First she felt as if someone were moving around the room in the dark. She stayed in bed telling herself it was only her imagination. Eventually the fatigue of a long day set in and she fell asleep.

She woke up at three o'clock.

She got a glass of water from her mini-fridge.

She sat in the dark on her bed and sipped her water.

And that's when she saw what she swears was the ghost of a teenage girl standing about three feet away from the edge of her bed.

"She had long, wavy brown hair and was wearing a long-sleeved nightgown," Denise said. "She was maybe five feet tall. She was hovering above the ground, leaning at an angle."

The ghost appeared to be solid but slightly transparent.

"You could see through the ghost's stomach to its back," Denise said. "It was solid but definitely 3-D."

The apparition hung beside her bed staring into the darkness as if she didn't see Denise sitting there on the edge of her bed holding that glass of water. She hung suspended in the darkness for only a few seconds. Still, Denise swears she got a good look at the spirit.

"I could have reached out and grabbed her," she said. "It's not like I was half-asleep or anything. I was wide awake."

Despite her interrupted sleep, Denise didn't seem one bit bothered by her visitation.

"I didn't feel like she was going to hurt me," she said. "Maybe next time I'll just say hi."

Why not? They say a body is supposed to meet new friends at university.

Robie Street

1714 ROBIE STREET

N 44°38.63′ W 63°35.33′

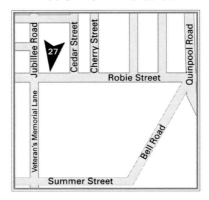

The Robie Street Witch's House

T HERE STANDS A HOUSE ON THE CORNER OF JUBILEE ROAD AND Robie Street that has long been thought to be haunted because of a single blackened window facing the street like the black and unreadable eye patch of a pirate. Some claim the window is cursed; others say the house was a victim of witchcraft.

Ask Any Cab Driver

It is one of the houses that children will dare each other to go up to on Halloween night. It is one of those houses that has a story or two that nearly everyone knows and no one can verify.

In short, it's a haunted house depending on whom you listen to. The house was originally built back in the 1940s for William Caldwell, the first elected mayor of Halifax. The house is built in a classic Greek symmetric style with three windows on each side. The middle window, facing out to Robie Street, is as black as midnight's darkest shade.

I first heard the story from a Halifax cab driver way back in the early 1970s when I first came to live in Halifax from my original home in Northern Ontario.

The Cab Driver's Story

"The place is haunted," he told me. "Haunted and cursed."

We drove by it slowly. It was a tall, pale white, and looming Doric structure with a single blackened window. It has been known at various times as the Century House, the Robie Street Palace and, of course, the Robie Street Witch's House.

I asked the cab driver to tell me what had happened to give this building such a bad reputation. If there's one thing I have found out over my years of rooting out stories is that if you ask any cab driver anything, he is bound to have a theory.

"It was curiosity that done it," the cabbie told me. "It seems this old guy used to live there and one night he looked out that window and he saw these witches dancing out on the front lawn of the house next door."

Now, I am married to a professional dancer and I have worked in the pagan community, so the sight of a band of dancing witches didn't sound like all that bad a fate to me.

However, the cab driver didn't stop there.

"They cursed him for being such a curious, nosy peeping Tom," he said. "They struck him blind and the window turned as black as fresh-poured pavement—like it had been painted with tar. They say that ever since that time the house owners have tried replacing the windowpane but it just turns black every time."

At which point, I paid my fare and tipped the man for a story well told.

The black strip on the left window of this Robie Street house gives it an ominous look.

The Second Story

However, there's a second story to the Robie Street Witch's House depending on whom you talk to.

Some folks will tell you that a previous owner had been having some trouble with a darned neighborhood kid stealing the cherries from his cherry tree. One morning he saw the boy climbing the tree and decided to give him a scare.

"That darned kid," the man said. "I'll fix him."

The man ran out with a shotgun full of rock salt and blasted a charge into the air thinking he would scare the boy with the noise. However, his plan worked all too well. The young boy was startled and fell from the tree and broke his neck. With the light dying slowly in his eyes, the boy died there in the man's arms. The man didn't even know the boy's name. He was just "that darned kid."

The man was devastated.

He went back inside and came back out with a rope in his hand. He tied a neat little hangman's noose and hanged himself from the cherry tree. As his feet kicked beneath him and life fled from his eyes, the young boy's dead body slowly cooled below his shadow. The window of the house from which he'd been watching slowly turned black, and it's been black to this day.

Or, at least that's how some people tell the story.

The Truth of the Matter

The true reason why the window is black is simply a matter of architecture. The window is black because it is nothing more than decorative. It was never meant to be looked through. Inside the house there is a wall directly behind the false window.

Some ghost stories aren't nearly as much fun when you look into them too closely. I, myself, far prefer to stare at a lawn full of dancing witches or even a couple of hairy-legged lawn gnomes in kilts.

The Cathedral Church of All Saints

5732 COLLEGE STREET

N 44°38.45' W 63°34.85'

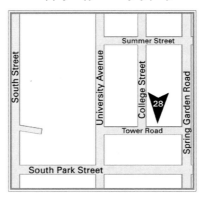

Unfinished Business

SINCE THE EARLY 1930S, THE CATHEDRAL CHURCH OF ALL SAINTS has been rumoured to be haunted by the ghostly spirit of the church's dean. His ghost has been seen by folks who knew him and folks who didn't, and sometimes at night a favourite hymn of his is still heard playing faintly in the cathedral.

Can't you hear the tune calling in the wind?

The History of the Cathedral

Stroll down Tower Road from the Robert Burns Memorial to College Street and you will find the Cathedral Church of All Saints, the seat of the Anglican bishop of both Nova Scotia and Prince Edward Island. Built from local granite quarried from across the Northwest Arm, the Cathedral Church of All Saints was officially opened on September 3, 1910. It survived damage from the Halifax Explosion of 1917 as well as several inherent design flaws.

The structure, repaired and renovated many times over the years, appears to be nearly immortal.

So it is no surprise to find out that the Cathedral Church of All Saints is haunted.

The Cathedral Church of All Saints on College Street is an impressive site, even half-covered with wispy fog.

Hurrying to Death's Doorway

It was a Sunday evening, January 1, 1933. You could smell the residue of gunpowder in the air from the shotguns, rifles, and fireworks that folks had fired off in the nighttime to celebrate the beginning of a brand-new year. People had hurried in that night to fling open their front and back doors in order to let the new year in and send the old year on its way.

It was a time of beginnings and endings and Dean John Plummer Derwent Llwyd was hurrying to death's doorway. A parishioner was ill, dying by all reports, and Dean Llwyd was determined to see the man off in a good and holy fashion.

It was the end of a very long day. Dean Llwyd had been up late to celebrate New Year's and then up early for Sunday morning mass. He stepped out from the doors of the cathedral humming his favourite hymn, "Come Down, O Love Divine." He was smiling softly to himself, happy in his chosen work.

He never saw the car that hit him.

He suffered a broken leg and someone else performed the last rites for his parishioner that night. A few short months later, Dean Llwyd passed away due to a blood clot that was directly caused by his broken leg.

He was twenty years old at the time of his death.

The Haunting

That very next Sunday following Dean Llwyd's untimely death, people attending services at the cathedral swear that they saw his ghost climbing calmly up the stairs to the pulpit as if to give his usual Sunday morning sermon. The floorboards and the wooden pillars that supported the collection plates shook discernibly as the organist played "Come Down, O Love Divine."

Oddly enough, no one felt afraid of the Dean Llwyd's presence.

"It was just as if the man wanted to be certain that everything was going on in its appointed way," one parishioner was heard to say.

This was only the first of many continued sightings. Since that day, the ghost of Dean Llwyd has been seen in the shadows of the cathedral going about his day-to-day routine as if nothing had ever changed.

I suspect his spirit is smiling softly to himself, happy in his chosen work.

Deadman's Island

24 PINEHAVEN DRIVE

N 44°38.00' W 63°36.55'

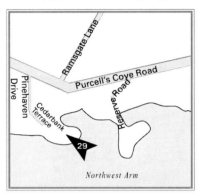

Still They Keep Watch

NTER DEADMAN'S ISLAND PARK AND YOU'LL SEE A PATH THAT leads you to the monument commemorating the island's fallen prisoners. But this "island" is actually a peninsula. Besides, the story doesn't even begin on Deadman's Island; it begins on Melville Island, which isn't an island anymore either since a causeway now links it to the shoreline. Melville Island is currently the home of the Armdale Yacht Club. To spot Melville Island, just look towards the west, where you will see a forest of masts. If you are facing the Deadman's Island monument, Melville Island is to your left.

During the War of 1812, American prisoners of war were held on Melville Island prison camp and buried on Deadman's Island after they died. Both islands (that aren't really islands) are said to be haunted by the ghosts of these prisoners.

It Reeked of Dead Fish

Melville Island was originally named Kavanagh Island after its owner, James Kavanagh, a merchant who ran a small but profitable fishing operation off Kavanagh Island. In 1793, as the Napoleonic War heated up in Europe and Halifax began getting ready for a French invasion that never arrived, prisoners captured from seized French vessels and from the islands of Saint-Pierre and Miquelon were primarily held in prison hulks—old ships, too old for sailing, that were turned into floating prisons.

Prison overcrowding and an increasing supply of POWs led Governor Wentworth to seek out a likely site for a new military prison. Kavanagh Island seemed a good spot. It was remote and cut off by the Atlantic. By 1795, Wentworth struck a deal with Kavanagh, and his two fish sheds were pressed into service as a makeshift military hospital and prison compound.

"The hospital reeked of dead fish," one prisoner was said to report. "Morning, noon, and night, I dream of cold kippers."

There's an old story my grandfather used to tell me about a farmer who takes pity on his plow horse and lets it poke its nose in the doorway of his house one cold winter night. Before too long, the horse is in the house and the farmer finds himself outside sleeping in the barn. That's just what happened with Kavanagh. He let the army get its snoot onto the island and he woke up out in the barn.

By 1803, with more prisoners to contend with than they had room for, the Admiralty made Kavanagh an offer—one thousand pounds for a property he'd paid sixty-five pounds for two decades back. The new owners renamed the island in honour of Viscount Melville, the newly appointed First Lord of the Admiralty, and Kavanagh took his fishing boat somewhere else.

Early Prison Life

In the early years of the prison, life was fairly comfortable. The majority of the prisoners were either French or Spanish. They got along well with their guards; some said they got along too well. The prisoners were clothed in bright, easily visible garb, and the letters POW were printed in dark red ink on the outside of their jackets, on the thigh of their trousers, and on the front and back of their shirts. The word *prisoner* was etched inside their shoes.

The prisoners were an industrious lot. Some of them brewed spruce beer and sold it to other prisoners and to the guards. Others performed laundry duties for prisoners and guards alike. They caught cod and mackerel; they made butter and candy. Some kept chickens or pigs and one man raised a kitten and trained it to dance and meow on command. He performed with the kitten for whatever small change the bystanders provided.

Many of the prisoners carved spoons and other small trinkets out of wood and ivory they bartered for. Once a week, citizens of Halifax visited the prison and a small makeshift marketplace soon arose. Occasionally prisoners were rewarded for good behaviour with a visit to a nearby pub. The visits came to a halt when a few prisoners got their captors handily drunk and snuck away in the night.

Another Escape Attempt

Strangely enough, there weren't many escape attempts. The French and Spanish enjoyed their comfortable prison life. It was a far better fate than what might have befallen them on the Napoleonic battlefield.

Of course, the guards did their duty well enough, and escape into the Nova Scotia wilderness, especially in the winter, did not tempt many. Besides, it was rumoured the guards kept a pet shark fed with fish scraps to keep it circling the island in order to discourage any maritime escapes. One wonders if it wasn't the guards who started the whole shark rumour in the first place.

Still, a few tried.

One cold winter, two homesick Frenchmen did their best to try to escape. Planning on escaping over the ice when the night finally fell, the two hid beneath one of the outhouses in the prison yard. However, when the evening roll was called, the two were missed. The guards searched and finally found them, cold and stinking, hiding in the privy hole and wishing for nothing but a return to their cells. For punishment they were put in the Black Hole—an iron-barred cell not much larger than the privy-hole they had escaped from—and they remained in their odorous garments for the rest of the night.

The two were kept in the hole for a week and were fed nothing but bread and water. The other prisoners reportedly ate only bread and water in sympathy for their daring comrades. While darned few of them wanted to chance the woods and the wilds surrounding Halifax, especially in the wintertime, they admired the courage and boldness such an attempt had taken.

The War of 1812

On June 18, 1812, the United States of America declared war on Great Britain and, therefore, Canada. This campaign brought a fresh supply of prisoners. The Melville Island prison facilities were put to the test as they took in nearly 1,800 prisoners at a time. The population was in a state of constant flux as prisoners were moved in, shipped out to England and further imprisonment, transferred to the prison hulks, or removed when they died.

The Canadian and British guards openly disliked this sudden rush of Americans. They didn't appreciate the overcrowding and didn't take kindly to the notion of somebody invading their country.

Conditions weren't comfortable anymore. The prison was cramped and disease-ridden. Some prisoners succumbed to wounds. Infectious disease took a steady toll as typhus, smallpox, pneumonia, and tuberculosis killed many.

The dead were rowed to the swampy peninsula then known as Target Hill and now called Deadman's Island. The guards sewed the dead up in shrouds of sailcloth making certain that the first and last stitch of thread went through the corpse's lip to be sure they weren't burying someone prematurely. They dug shallow graves, kept their prayers short, and cursed their aching backs.

Death, the shroud, and a shallow grave: between 1812 and 1813, over eight thousand American prisoners of war were funnelled through Melville Island's prison camp and nearly two hundred of them found a final resting place on Deadman's Island.

The war ended with the signing of the Treaty of Ghent on December 24, 1814, but fifty more American prisoners of war died in the three months it took for the news of the treaty to reach Nova Scotia.

Melville Island and the burial ground on Deadman's Island continued to turn a lively trade. Refugee slaves from the United States were confined here through the two years following the War of 1812. From 1818 to 1847, the prison camp served as a quarantine hospital. The camp served as a British military prison from 1856 to 1905. And finally, the island facilities were used as a prison camp for German prisoners through both world wars.

And over those years, a lot more bodies were buried on Deadman's Island.

The peninsula known as Deadman's Island is located in Halifax's Northwest Arm.

The Dead Find Rest

"There have always been all kinds of sinister stories about the island," said Brian Cuthbertson, a Halifax historian. "Tales of bones coming to surface, of graves unearthed by storms, of people chancing upon skulls."

The ghosts of those forgotten prisoners of war have been seen time and again on the shores of Deadman's Island. Local home builders have dug up skulls while digging their house foundations. Dogs loved to run free on the island and dig up their own kind of buried treasure. It became a common double-dare for kids to dare other kids to pitch a tent on Deadman's Island or, worse yet, take a shovel and dig for bones.

Still, it was a pretty piece of land with ocean frontage to boot. It was only a matter of time before Halifax developers turned the sights of their earth-moving machines on Deadman's Island. In 1999, local developers decided to build a massive condominium complex on the island.

A group of local historians banded together and proved that all of the stories of bones being found on Deadman's Island were true. The Royal Canadian Legion waded into the battle as well. Then, when a United States veterans association got into the fight and pressed the US Congress to use some of its influence with the Canadian government, the tide finally turned.

In 2000, the owner of the property sold it to the municipality of Halifax and in 2003, Deadman's Island, which included the bones of over 400 lost souls buried there, was finally recognized as a brand-new, official historic park.

On May 30, 2007, Memorial Day for the Americans, a monument was erected and dedicated honouring the fallen prisoners of war of Deadman's Island. The commemoration and blessing were performed by Padre Lieutenant Commander David Schilling, a representative from the US, and Padre Lieutenant (Navy) Jack Barret, a Canadian representative.

The old prison still stands on Melville Island, directly by the water's edge, and now serves to provide storage for the yachting club's boating equipment. On quiet summer nights, many local yacht owners have seen shapes moving through the shadows and have heard strange

This monument stands to honour all the fallen prisoners of Deadman's Island.

sounds in the woods. Of course, that might just be the wind talking with the waves.

One can only hope that finally once and for all, the ghosts of Deadman's Island can rest in peace.

Ashburn Golf Club (The Old Course)

3250 JOSEPH HOWE DRIVE
N 44°39.03' W 63°37.85'

A Strange Old Lady

THE ASHBURN GOLF CLUB IS REPUTED TO BE HAUNTED BY THE ghost of an old woman who once lived there. She has been seen, time and again, by all kinds of startled golfers.

I suspect she's still out there perhaps searching for her missing husband or perhaps that elusive hole in one.

The Story

According to the club's promotional material, the Ashburn Golf Club has been an integral part of the Halifax landscape since Governor General Lord Byng drove the very first ceremonial ball from the first tee of the Old Course in 1923.

However, the golf course is apparently haunted.

An article written by E. Wetmore and published in the pages of a March 1954 edition of the *Mail-Star* tells that a late-summer visitor walking the golf course in the late 1930s encountered an old woman in a long, flowing shawl the colour of burnt umber.

Not strange enough for you yet?

It seems the old woman had no feet at all. Her legs seemingly ended at her ankle bones. Stranger yet was the fact that the old woman was actually hovering about two or three inches above the grass.

"She had no shadow as far as I could tell," the witness reported. "And she just sort of hung there as if she were suspended upon a rope of some sort."

The witness tried to approach her, but she wrapped the shawl about her head as if she were hiding from something. She waved her free hand wildly in the air clearly indicating that she did not wish to be disturbed.

"I couldn't help feeling that she needed my help," the witness went on. "I tried to get closer to her but she glided into the woods and vanished."

Glided.

Vanished.

Strange choice of words, don't you think?

A Possible Explanation

When the story got out, the golf course owners were quick to investigate.

It seems that this eerie spectral woman was the ghost of an old widow who had been found dead. According to local residents the widow lived on Dutch Village Road just across from the golf course's entrance.

She lived there with her son and daughter-in-law. Apparently she had never been the same since she lost her husband suddenly. He had been struck with a heart attack in the middle of a golf game.

The haunted trees of the Ashburn Golf Club

As a direct result, his old wife suffered from melancholy and bouts of dementia and would often be found wandering through her neighbour's yards and up and down her street or into the golf course where her husband had loved to play.

One cold late-summer morning, she wandered into an ash grove on the golf course and twisted her shawl about her neck and hanged herself from the branch of one of the tallest ash trees. She was found a day later; her feet were dangling just a few inches from the ground and crows were circling above her over the branches.

Folks still see her every now and then. She always looks a little panicked as if she's lost. Some describe her as a little angry as if she were upset that her husband went and died without asking her permission. Still, she's never harmed anyone or given any sign that she might want to.

I have looked for details and asked some folks at Ashburn just where on the course this whole thing might have happened, but the details have been lost to time and tale-telling. Nevertheless, folks say that the leaves of the ash grove turn the shade of burnt umber in the late summer as autumn begins her long, lonely walk towards winter.

Fairview Lawn Cemetery

WINDSOR STREET AND KEMPT ROAD

N 44°39.66' W 63°37.45'

The Dead of the *Titanic*

HERE ARE SEVERAL STRANGE STORIES TOLD ABOUT THE FAIRVIEW
Lawn Cemetery, particularly concerning the ship-shaped site of
the burial place of 121 of the victims of the sinking of the *Titanic*.
To see the graves, enter the cemetery and follow the signs around to the
burial site—the way to the *Titanic* site is clearly marked.

An Inauspicious Beginning

The *Titanic*'s first and only voyage began under less than auspicious circumstances. As it steamed out of the port of Southampton, England, the suction generated by the combination of its sheer mass and the churning of its massive propeller blades snapped the seven steel hawser cables that kept the 10,500-ton ocean liner *New York* safely moored.

The *New York* drifted free and, drawn by the irresistible pull of the current, nearly rammed the *Titanic* before it had even cleared the harbour. Only the quick action of the tugboats *Vulcan* and *Neptune* saved the *Titanic* from a near-crippling collision.

In hindsight, one wonders if it might not have been better for all if the tugboat captains had not been quite so quick thinking.

Three Strikes Are All You Get

Mind you, it wasn't like it was much of an even match.

The *Titanic* measured 883 feet in length—almost one-sixth of a mile. It weighed in at 46,328 tons, or over four times the weight of the wayward *New York*. At the time it was built, the *Titanic* was said to be the largest man-made movable object in history.

The *Titanic* sailed out of Southampton, picked up additional passengers in Cherbourg, France and Queenstown, Ireland, and steamed for New York City. It was sailing under the command of Captain E. J. Smith, a long-time veteran of the White Star Line—the owners of the *Titanic*. By Sunday, April 14, 1912, Captain Smith believed he had the voyage well under control. The sea was dead calm, the weather was comfortably cold, and the ship was making good time.

"Perhaps we will make New York City a day early," the captain predicted.

The radio crew was bogged down with a backlog of passenger messages for home. Clearing the message backlog kept the radio crew busy enough to overlook a warning of icebergs ahead.

A second message was sent but was delivered to the bridge while the captain was at lunch. Both that message and a third warning were misplaced by the overworked radio crew. The *Titanic* continued onward, unaware of the icefields ahead. The ship pushed its speed from twenty-one knots up to twenty-five.

Three chances were all they were going to get.

A Blue Iceberg

In the spring of 1912, a strangely mild winter pushed an inordinately large mass of ice floes down into the Labrador current. The most dangerous of these ice floes were known as "blue icebergs." A blue iceberg is an iceberg that has recently turned end-over-end in the water exposing a massive waterlogged underbelly so dark blue in color that the iceberg is nearly invisible during the hours of night. It was just such a blue iceberg that sank the *Titanic* on the morning hours of April 15, 1912.

About twenty minutes before midnight, the lookouts, Frederick Fleet and Reginald Lee, spotted a patch of thick fog ahead of them. By the time the *Titanic* closed to just a few hundred feet from the oncoming fog bank, a lookout spotted the blue iceberg just beyond the fog bank.

First Officer William Murdoch, acting commander in the wheelhouse while the captain was in bed, reacted quickly to the crisis at hand.

"Full speed astern," he ordered.

The engine room crew backed as hard as they could. However, much as the *Imo* would find out as it attempted to back from its collision with the *Mont Blanc* five years later, momentum carried the *Titanic* straight towards the oncoming iceberg.

"Hard a-starboard," Murdoch ordered, trying to turn the *Titanic* around the iceberg.

Unfortunately, the attempt was futile. There was no way they could turn the ship fast enough. Murdoch sounded the crash alarm and closed the watertight emergency doors down below. The unsinkable *Titanic* ground hard against the iceberg, tearing open nearly the entire length of the ship's starboard bow.

Awoken by the impact and noise, Captain Smith rushed onto the bridge too late to save his mighty vessel.

Women and Children First

Five minutes after midnight, the *Titanic* sent out distress calls and readied its lifeboats for dispersal. A half an hour later, the first lifeboat was lowered into the Atlantic.

"We are putting women and children off in boats," the *Titanic* radioed. Over an hour later, the last lifeboat left the *Titanic*.

Consider the arithmetic. On its maiden voyage, the *Titanic* carried a total of 1,316 passengers and a crew of 913 all told. The ship was equipped with a total of twenty lifeboats. It was originally designed to carry thirty-two lifeboats, but the White Star Line decided the number of lifeboats needed to be reduced to twenty in order not to spoil the vessel's clean and streamlined appearance.

Each lifeboat had a capacity to carry fifty passengers and a crew of eight sailors to operate it safely. However, in the rush, most of the lifeboats that were launched were carrying a fair bit less than their maximum capacity.

Four of the lifeboats were damaged irrevocably during the evacuation.

At 2:18 AM on April 15, 1912, the lights blinked once on the *Titanic* before the ship fell into darkness. Shortly thereafter it broke in two and its bow immediately sank.

Its stern half tipped upwards like a monolithic steel tombstone looming over the lifeboats before slipping beneath the waves to plunge nearly 3,000 fathoms straight down to the bottom of the ocean, about 700 miles from Halifax Harbour.

Of the 2,229 human souls aboard the *Titanic*, only 713 were saved.

The survivors were picked up by the liner *Carpathia* and taken to New York.

It was up to Halifax to gather up the dead.

The Death Ship

Halifax rallied into action. Coffins were loaded aboard the *Mackay-Bennett*, a vessel designed for laying and repairing transatlantic underwater cable. The ship's cranes and hoists would be put to a far darker use than the original designer ever imagined.

John Snow and Company, Nova Scotia's largest undertaking business, was given the task of seeing to the burial preparations. A wire for help went out through the Maritimes. Forty embalmers travelled to Halifax to assist. The only female embalmer present, Annie F. O'Neil of Saint John, New Brunswick, would embalm the women and children who had missed the lifeboats.

Over a hundred crude, wooden coffins were loaded. Tins of embalming fluid, tons of ice, burlap sacks, and barrels full of cogs and horseshoes and scrap iron to weigh down the sacks of those who were to be buried at sea were brought on board.

Captain F. H. Lardner was in command. His entire crew of seventy-five had volunteered for this duty, but he saw to it that they would receive double pay for the grisly business ahead. Canon Kenneth Hinds of Halifax's Cathedral Church of All Saints was also on board to perform any necessary spiritual duties and to see to the burial of those whose bodies were too sea-worn to be returned to Halifax.

The *Mackey-Bennett* set sail on Wednesday, April 17, two days after the sinking. This ship was travelling at full speed when it left Halifax Harbour, but fog and poor weather slowed its progress. They reached the fateful spot three days later and dropped anchor at eight o'clock at night planning to wait until the morning to begin their search. All evening long the crew waited, trying not to brood over the icebergs still surrounding the area and the smaller, darker shapes drifting about their vessel.

"The ocean was covered, as far as the eye can see, with remains and corpses which rolled on the water like stoppers," wrote crewman Arminias Wiseman.

The system of retrieval was simple. A tag of canvas was attached to each body with a stencilled number representing the order in which it was found. The fourth body was a small, fair-haired boy who looked to be about two years old.

"He came floating towards us with a little upturned face," John Snow reported afterwards. The child had neither a life belt nor identification papers. Snow believed that the child's natural baby fat had helped keep his small body buoyant in the heavy Atlantic waves. They named him the "Unknown Child."

The Hierarchy of Death

There were 325 first-class passengers, 285 second-class passengers, and 706 third-class passengers on board the *Titanic* when it hit the iceberg. There were also a few stowaways and unverifiable passengers not listed in the liner's roll.

Each body was carefully searched for valuables and identification. First-class bodies were immediately embalmed and placed in coffins. Second-class passengers were embalmed if there was time, but otherwise they were packed into burlap shrouds. Third-class passengers were primarily stacked on ice. Corpses too mangled for identification were bundled in burlap, weighted with iron, and buried at sea. All told, the *Mackay-Bennett* picked up a total of 306 bodies and buried 116 of them at sea.

A second ship, the *Minia*, was dispatched with additional embalming fluid, burlap and iron, twenty tons of ice, and a fresh supply of 150 coffins. The coffins had been manufactured by the James Dempster Company Ltd. following an all-day double shift in the casket factory. The *Minia* rendezvoused with the *Mackay-Bennett* as a third ship, the *Montmagny*, set out for the death grounds.

On return to Halifax, the victims were taken by carriage to the Mayflower Curling Rink on Agricola Street (now the site of Ron's Army and Navy Surplus), which had been hastily equipped to serve as a makeshift mass morgue.

Following a two-week holding period which gave relatives time to arrange to pick up some of the bodies for transfer, a final mass burial was arranged. Nineteen of the bodies were buried at the Mount Olivet Roman Catholic Cemetery at the corner of Mumford Road and Olivet Street. Ten other *Titanic* victims were buried at the Baron de Hirsch Jewish Cemetery on the corner of Connaught Avenue and Windsor Street.

However, it is the 121 victims buried in the Fairview Lawn Cemetery that hold the most interest for the seeker of eerie tales.

Fairview Lawn Cemetery

The Fairview Lawn Cemetery is located in the North End of Halifax at the intersection of Windsor Street and Kempt Road. You'll have to drive here; this is one ghost tour site that is definitely too far to walk. The *Titanic* site is marked clearly with a large white sign that simply reads "Titanic."

This long line of tombstones is just part of the of the massive burial grounds for the Titanic *victims at the Fairview Lawn Cemetery.*

Each grave is individually numbered. The number represents the order in which the person buried there was hauled from out of the Atlantic. The tombstones are laid out in the shape of a ship's bow. There is a gap on the starboard—or right hand side—precisely where the *Titanic* struck the iceberg. Whether this gap is intentional or simply a coincidence is not known.

Party poopers and other practical folk will tell you that the shape of the burial site was simply a result of the fact that the gravediggers plowed a large trench in the dirt and laid the bagged bodies out side by side before covering them up. There were simply too many corpses to deal with digging individual graves. So the ship's outline that you see might be nothing more than the mark of the plow.

Stranger yet is that some people believe that the outline of the ship, as formed by the gravestones, is facing in the same compass direction as the wreck of the *Titanic* was facing when it was finally discovered in 1985.

The Unknown Child

The fourth victim removed from the Atlantic waters was an unknown boy of about two years of age. Following a solemn funeral ceremony conducted at St. George's Round Church, where the coffin of the unknown child was carried into the church upon the shoulders of the crew of the *Mackay-Bennett*, the child was buried in Fairview Lawn Cemetery. He is buried close to what would be the bow of the ship and his grave is marked by a tall square pillar.

A headstone was erected with the following inscription: "Erected to the memory of an Unknown Child whose remains were recovered after the disaster of the *Titanic*, April 15, 1912."

For years afterwards, tourists and travellers would visit the *Titanic* gravesite here in the Fairview Lawn Cemetery and leave small toys and stuffed animals on the gravestone of the unknown child.

For a long time it was believed that the unknown child was none other than Gosta Paulson, whose mother, Alma Paulson, was buried just a few feet away. However, following DNA testing of the few scraps of bone and teeth that remained, it was announced in the July 2004 issue of *American Cemetery Magazine* that the unknown child actually was Eino Viljam Panula, age thirteen months and originally from Finland. But in 2007, Canadian researchers ascertained through further testing that the unidentified child's DNA did not match the Panula family. Eventually, a DNA match was found and the unknown child was identified as Sidney Leslie Goodwin, a 19-month-old passenger from England.

In spite of the confirmed identification, the unknown child remains buried in the Fairview Lawn Cemetery beneath his original gravestone. The tombstone inscription remains as a grim quiet monument to the fifty-three young children who died when the *Titanic* sank. Most of

The tombstone at the Titanic gravesite marked J. Dawson is often honoured as being the grave of the fictional Jack Dawson in James Cameron's Titanic.

their bodies were never found, but their memory lingers onward in the quiet expanse of the Fairview Lawn Cemetery.

The Mystery of J. Dawson

Perhaps the most famous Fairview Lawn Cemetery *Titanic* gravestone belongs to a twenty-three-year-old coal trimmer named Joseph Dawson. A trimmer had the rough job of fetching coal from the various coal stations in the belly of the ship to make certain that the loads were evenly distributed so as to keep the ship on "trim"—that is, even in the water.

Since the 1997 release of Canadian-born writer and director James Cameron's movie *Titanic*, young romantic souls have been making a pilgrimage to the gravesite of Joseph Dawson, or as it states on the tombstone—"J. Dawson"—to lay bouquets of flowers and movie ticket stubs and small coins as a tribute to Leonardo DiCaprio's character in the film, Jack Dawson. Dawson's stone lies in the third row of tombstones, eleven stones from the left, number 227.

Now I want to make it clear that Jack Dawson is a fictitious character invented by James Cameron in order to help move the plotline of his wonderful movie forward. And I also want to make it clear that I may actually have shed a tear or two as poor Jack Dawson met his cinematic fate. Nonetheless, he isn't real.

Real or not, I will bet you lonely young girls will be placing coins and mementoes and theatre tickets on his tombstone for as long as folks remember the *Titanic*.

Prince's Lodge

BEDFORD HIGHWAY

N 44°41.45' W 63°39.569'

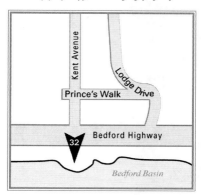

A Duel That Will Not Die

O FIND PRINCE'S LODGE, TRAVEL DOWN THE BEDFORD HIGHWAY until you come to the intersection where Kent Avenue (on the left-hand side) meets up with Bedford Highway. There, nestled on the coast between the iron ribbon of the railway and the waiting waters of the Bedford Basin, stands the Prince's Lodge. It's a privately-owned residence that used to be home to royalty. In July 1798, a deadly duel was fought upon its grounds and the spirit of one of the duellists has been seen walking through the area, brandishing his sword, and perhaps looking for a second chance to thrust the blade home.

A Prince Arrives in Halifax

Boney was a warrior, away-ay-ya.
A warrior, a tarrier, Jean François.

The Russians have a saying: "Love is like a war. Easy to begin but hard to end."

Prince Edward, the Duke of Kent, knew just what those old Russians were talking about. He had a love for architecture, a love for engineering, a love for the military, and a love for Madame Julie St. Laurent.

Of these four loves, three would last his lifetime.

In the year of 1793, a French artillery captain by the name of Napoleon Bonaparte began his rise to power as France went to war against the united allies of Spain, Italy, the Netherlands, and Great Britain.

One year later, Prince Edward, a soldier and a son of King George III, sailed into Halifax hot from a brief but glorious campaign in the West Indies. He was a young man burning to build himself a reputation, and he had become obsessed with the notion that sooner or later revolutionary France would lead its armies across the Atlantic and straight down the mouth of Halifax Harbour.

He landed at King's Wharf to a rousing twenty-one gun salute and promptly demanded and received the position of Nova Scotia's acting commander-in-chief. He certainly thought he was a hot commodity as he roared into Halifax like Davy Crockett barrelling into the Alamo, King Leonidas striding into the Hot Gates, or General Custer riding into the Little Big Horn. And then, like a young man set loose in a room full of Lego toys, Prince Edward began to build.

He set to work on rebuilding the Citadel and the fort on George's Island. He laid a huge chain across the Harbour and anchored it at a rock in Point Pleasant Park that is still known as Chain Rock. He set up the first working semaphore telegraph system in North America. He improved harbour defences, scaled up the artillery batteries, and set his finest engineers and construction men to work on raising three Martello towers—one in Point Pleasant Park, one on the Eastern Battery, and one on the slopes of York Redoubt.

He was a bit of a Tim Allen that way. He had ideas, most of them sound ones, that were based on architecture and armaments and harbour defence and love. Oh my yes, Prince Edward had his own ideas of love.

You see, Prince Edward was madly in love with a mistress, Madame Alphonsine Thérèse Bernardine Julie de Montgenet de St. Laurent, Baronne de Fortisson—a young widow, an aristocrat in her own country, and a lady with a history as long as her full name. Edward kept her and loved Julie with all of his heart even though he knew that someday he would have to marry a royal bride, and a widowed French noblewoman—no matter how heart-achingly beautiful she was—sadly did not fill the bill.

And that's the pain of it. He knew he would not keep her forever. He could not, if he hoped to ever gain the crown, and Prince Edward certainly wanted the crown. Julie very likely knew it as well. But he would keep her for as long as he could in as fine a surrounding as she had ever dreamed of.

A Lover's Hideaway

Edward built his sugar shack for Julie on the shores of the Bedford Basin where the Lodge now stands. He built his love a house—a two-storey, wooden building framed in the Italian style—with wings at each end and a grand hall and reception room directly in the centre. He stocked the library with as many books as he could manage to collect—no easy task in that day and age. He lost an entire library to one shipwreck off Sable Island but replaced it with another shipment a year later. Being a prince had its perks.

Edward had the offensive undergrowth cleared and trimmed and pruned and he had white gravel pathways laid out that spelled out Julie's name. His builders erected Chinese pagodas and Greek temples. The centrepiece was a carefully crafted rotunda built for music and dancing and long private talks.

That rotunda is the only structure that has survived the years. Built to withstand the siege of time and lost love, the rotunda can be seen from the Bedford Highway and looks like a miniature Martello tower. Just

This rotunda is the only remnant left of Prince Edward's lodge.

travel down the Bedford Highway, past Mount St. Vincent University, through the Rockingham District, and just a little beyond Birch Cove and you will see it perched there on the hillside directly across from Kent Avenue, with the Bedford Basin at its back and the railroad tracks running between it and the highway.

It was a beautiful little spot. The original owner of the property, Governor Wentworth, called the haven "Friar Lawrence's Cell," thinking of *Romeo and Juliet*. He didn't know how truly prophetic his words would be.

Prince Edward had his soldiers and labourers carve out grottoes and dig a heart-shaped fish pond. He also had them lay out a fine picnic ground, construct a private barracks to house an entire company of the Royal Nova Scotia Regiment, and erect a semaphore-telegraph station in order to assure his love's perfect safety.

All was picture-postcard perfect.

However, there was a darker side to this story.

Three Lonely Graves

No one knows if she was truly happy; however, one thing was for certain—Julie St. Laurent loved to party. She was a charming hostess and Prince Edward would invite the leaders of the Halifax social elite to party and mingle on the basin's shore.

It was during one of these parties that tragedy struck. In July 1798, Prince Edward and Madame St. Laurent were hosting a party with at least three hundred officers and guests enjoying the wonderful summer weather. The grounds were lit by hundreds of lanterns hung from the branches of the hemlock trees and a regiment band provided the music.

Although it seemed to be a picture of beauty and serenity, not everyone was in the mood to party. A Colonel Ogilvie and a Captain Howard argued and it was decided that a duel of honour was the only way to settle the dispute. Ogilvie and Howard squared off for battle in front of the rotunda.

"*En garde*," Ogilvie said.

The two officers placed their sabres hilt to hilt. Howard made the first move—a clumsy swing. He was a naval officer who was used to wielding a heavy cutlass, and the brandy he'd indulged in sure didn't help much either. Ogilvie was an experienced swordsman and he parried Howard's awkward swing with an ease that made the captain appear quite foolish. The spectators laughed at Howard's clumsiness.

That laugh didn't help matters much. Humiliation and enthusiasm can beat the heck out of duelling technique. Howard smashed aside Ogilvie's next parry, carving a pot roast-sized slice out of Ogilvie's rib cage. Ogilvie fell to his knees, futilely pressing his splayed palm across the wound.

"That'll teach you," Howard said with a cold smile. He turned away.

That was Howard's last mistake.

Ogilvie instinctively brought his sabre up for a final thrust, driving the blade point first into the small of Howard's back. It proved to be Ogilvie's last act upon this earth. Ogilvie crashed face first into the gravel path, smearing the pristine white gravel with his own blood.

Howard's comrades caught him before he fell.

"I'm wounded," Howard said.

That was an understatement. He was bleeding out and no one could save him. Captain Howard died before they could carry him into the rotunda. It was probably just as well. He would have only left a stain upon Madame St. Laurent's pinewood floorboards. When Howard's friends saw that the man was dead, they panicked and left him lying on the steps of the rotunda.

Prince Edward was furious. He ordered Howard buried where he lay without military honour or ceremony. The fun was over, the party finished, and what had started as a society soiree degenerated into a seedy funeral.

A short time following the unfortunate duel, Edward was thrown by his favourite stallion. The horse broke its leg in the fall. Edward shot the horse where it lay. Those who knew the prince swore he loved that horse as much as he loved Julie.

Perhaps he did.

He had the horse buried in one of the quieter grottoes. The grave took a little longer to dig than the unfortunate Captain Howard's had taken, but what else are soldiers for? Edward decided it was a good idea to close the Prince's Lodge until happier times.

Julie, however, wished to stay on right where she was happiest. Prince Edward bowed to her wishes and allowed her to stay in the Prince's Lodge. He knew where he had to be. He had been ordered back to London to marry the Princess of Lenningen.

The party was over.

Julie St. Laurent learned of this marriage through a several-week-old newspaper article. She left the lodge and entered a convent where some years later she quietly pined away. Her heart was broken. That it stopped beating was nothing short of a mercy.

Following that fateful duel between Ogilvie and Howard, a ghostly figure wrapped in a military cloak has been seen pacing back and forth to the south of the rotunda just short of where the railroad tracks now run. Some people swear they have seen a large ghostly stallion galloping into the waves.

Bruce Nunn writes about an actual eyewitness to the ghost of Prince's Lodge in his story collection *History with a Twist*. In it he interviews a young man who lived in a house that was situated fairly close to the rotunda. The young man swears that he awoke at two o'clock one morning to see an eerie spectre dressed in an old military uniform standing at the foot of his bed.

"He had his hand on a sword handle protruding from the front of his cloak, and he had the most intensely angry look I have ever seen on a person's face."

Was it the spirit of the vengeful Captain Howard?

Perhaps.

Or possibly it was the spirit of Edward searching for his long-lost love?

However, the longer I think on it I have to wonder if maybe the real ghost of Prince's Lodge isn't a prince or a horse or a ham-handed duellist but rather a lonely young woman by the name of Julie St. Laurent who loved one man so intensely that she couldn't live without him.

I'm only guessing, you understand, but my storytelling heart will accept no other possibility. Mind you, no one has ever seen Julie's ghost nor has anyone ever claimed to truly know the depths of her feelings. Not even the clever Prince Edward had any idea how deep a woman's love could truly run. Perhaps it ran as deep and eternal as the Atlantic Ocean that separated the Prince's Lodge from Buckingham Palace.

Navy Island

BEDFORD BASIN

N 44°41.91' W 63°37.17'

A Changing of the Guard

I F YOU COULD THROW A ROCK ACROSS THE BEDFORD BASIN FROM Prince's Lodge you might hit Navy Island. The island rests in the shelter of a small cove that is also the home of the Dartmouth Yacht Club. A long drive to Dartmouth and down Windmill Road will get you there, but you can just as easily observe the island from Prince's Lodge and save yourself a trip. A story is just a stone's throw away.

Folks who live along the Bedford Basin will tell you that you can hear the eerie slap and splash of muffled oars and the grunts and curses of straining men on foggy nights out on the basin water. That isn't much of a story, but I hunted hard to find this tale of pirate's treasure that might just explain the whole business about folks hearing the sound of oar-splashing.

Steven's Island

Navy Island.

It's not much to look at—just a lozenge-shaped island off the Bedford Basin in the mouth of Wrights Cove. You can see it from the Dartmouth Yacht Club off Windmill Road and Akerley Boulevard, directly beyond the yachts. It is hard to miss, neatly sheltering the moored yachts from the waters of the Bedford Basin. Frankly, it sort of looks like a really big dog left a nasty mess behind and somebody planted some pine trees on top of it.

The island plays hide and seek with the tide. When the tide is high you see two islands, but when the tide is low you can see that the two islands are actually joined by a sandbar. It is the larger island that is most generally referred to as Navy Island.

There isn't much to this island; it's nothing more than a few ruined cottages and campsites. It isn't all that hard to get to. A good canoeist might be able to reach it and camp there. In the past they called it Steven's Island or Glassey's Island. I haven't been able to find who Steven or Glassey were, so if any readers have a notion I'd be glad to hear from you.

Like most Maritime islands, there are a lot of stories attached to Navy Island. Some swear one of Duc d'Anville's ill-fated fleet ran aground on Navy Island back in 1746. Others claim the island was a site for naval gunnery practice in the late sixties. There is talk of a trading post, an ancient First Peoples' graveyard, and a fishing station where fishermen dried their cod. Most of this is hearsay, or so I've heard, but the story I want to tell involves a young sailor, a boat full of pirates, and a cache of secret buried treasure.

Rowing Practice

Let's take ourselves back to a calm and very hot summer day in July 1825. There's a small flotilla of four British frigates moored in the calm safety of the Bedford Basin. There isn't a breath of wind stirring. It's what the sailors call a slick sea; it's dishwater calm and hot enough to fry spit. We're talking hot weather—dreary and slow.

A view of Bedford Basin from Navy Island

The day slid by like a molasses-fed snail. A young, off-duty midshipman by the name of Jamie Bryson asked the officer on duty for permission to take one of the ship's boats out for a short row.

"Just a row around the basin, sir," young Jamie said.

"That seems like hot work to me, son. You'd better stay here in the cool."

Jamie just grinned.

"If there's any cool out here on this water," he said. "I'll have to row it down and catch it."

The officer considered the matter.

"A fishing trip, is it?"

"Rowing practice, sir," Jamie said. "Just blowing the stink off."

That made sense to the lieutenant. He had half a mind to join the young midshipman, but that would have certainly involved a gross dereliction of an officer's duty. So instead he decided to let him have his way.

"A capital idea," the Lieutenant said. "Be sure you're back by nightfall. There's a fog creeping round out there beyond the basin and it'll steal in here soon enough."

Stick in the Mud

Jamie Bryson rowed strongly until the heat got to him.

He upped the oars and let the boat drift. He leaned back, enjoying the feel of the sun upon his upturned face. It wasn't any cooler, even down this close to the sea level, but free was free. It just felt fine being this far away from duty and the ship.

Bryson dozed off and dreamed of mermaids singing to him in soft, rushing whispers. A surreptitious eddy coaxed the midshipman's boat in towards the shore of Navy Island and shoaled up on the mudflat until the boat was completely aground.

Bryson woke up, chilled to the bone, which concerned him more than running aground. The tide would turn and he could easily get his boat back into the water. For now he was cold. He'd rowed himself into a lather and then a fog had rolled in and cooled the sweat on his skin.

A flock of goosebumps gaggled along his back and shoulders.

"Brrr," he said. "The weather sure turned off some fast."

He was complaining for something to do. The truth of it was he'd had plenty of experience with Nova Scotia weather, which could turn from warm as fair to cold as fish in half a blow. The fog would lift and the chill would pass, so he busied himself dragging the boat up to the shore of the island.

"A walk's what I need," he said. "Stretch my legs and get the blood flowing."

He did his best not to think about the trouble he would be in when he returned late to his vessel. He could see the wreckage of what looked to be the ruins of an old defence post. He figured he'd make for that and start a fire in the lea of the fallen walls. Perhaps his shipmates would spot the smoke and fetch him back.

"Halloo!" a voice called out from the fog before Bryson could get any closer to the ruins.

"Here ahoy!" Bryson shouted back. Perhaps the lieutenant had sent a search crew out for him. That could be a good thing or a bad thing depending on how much trouble the lieutenant felt he'd been.

"Halloo," the voice repeated.

Bryson was about to call again when someone called out in reply.

"Halloo the boat," the second voice called.

Bryson looked around. He'd thought that the island was deserted, but the second voice seemed to come from the ruins. He stumbled closer and was amazed to see a small campfire blazing in the heart of the ruined defence post. A sailor stood there, warming his hands by the fire.

"Hello the camp," Bryson said.

The sailor didn't seem to notice Bryson's approach, but the fire was too inviting to ignore. Bryson stepped closer. He could see the sailor clearly now. He was dressed strangely—wearing wide old-fashioned trousers, long sealskin boots, and a pea jacket with exaggerated cuffs and shiny brass buttons. He wore a large leather belt and sported a pair of wide-mouthed pistols, several evilly hooked daggers, and a cutlass. His hair was tied back into a tight braid that looked to have been tarred and singed like old sailors would have worn.

The man's attire was strange; yet, his appearance was even stranger. As Bryson drew closer, he could see the flames of the campfire flickering through the flesh of the man as if he were made of nothing more substantial than thin, tattered sailcloth.

A ghost.

Bryson's blood froze in his veins.

And then things got even worse. He heard the splash of oars out to sea. A boat was being dragged up onto the shore of the little island. A group of equally ragged spirits clambered out of the boat and made their way up to the campfire.

Bryson crouched down keeping his mouth closed. He tried to hold his breath, fearful that this band of phantoms might find him out and work some unholy and unworldly act of vengeance upon him.

One of the figures approached the ghostly watchman. He seemed taller than the rest and wore a fine tri-corner hat upon his head. Bryson guessed him to be the captain.

"How long?" the captain asked.

"Forty years," the watchman replied.

"And forty years more," the captain said.

Then the band of ghostly pirates turned and made its way back out into the sea, and the phantom watchman merely turned back to the fire and stood there alone, his shoulders slightly slumped.

Once the sound of their muffled oar splash was past his earshot, Bryson made his own way back to his boat. He pushed off from the island and spent the rest of the night adrift upon the waves.

He didn't sleep a wink.

In the morning he found his way back to his vessel. The lieutenant was waiting as was the captain. Bryson did his best to explain, but of course no one believed his story. They figured he'd found himself a bottle of rum and had dreamed the whole thing up.

The captain had Bryson flogged—the usual punishment for desertion of duties—and Bryson thanked him loudly at every crack of the whip. There were worse fates than flogging, he imagined.

Forty years and forty years more.